# MAGICAL TWIST

## MAGICAL WITCHERY BOOK 3

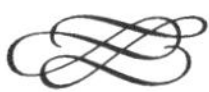

BRENDA TRIM

Editor: Chris Cain
Cover Art by Fiona Jayde

* * *



Created with Vellum

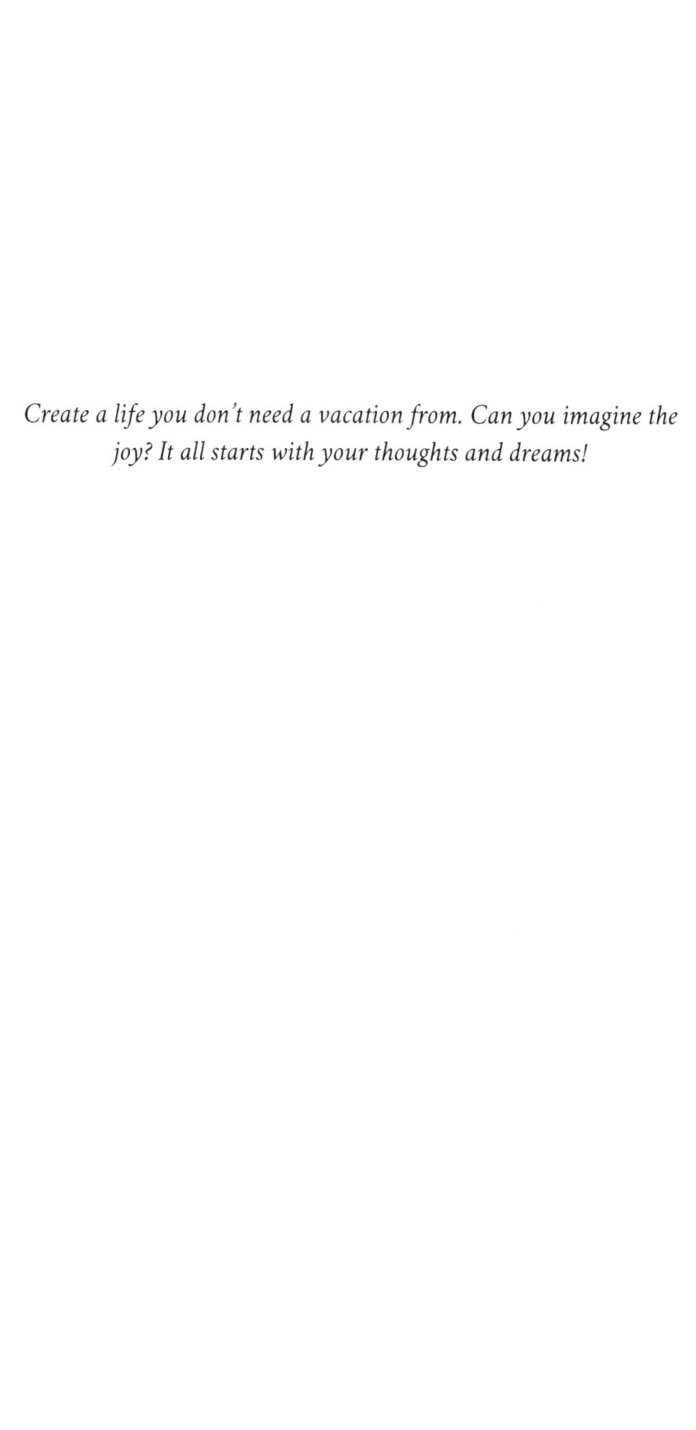

*Create a life you don't need a vacation from. Can you imagine the joy? It all starts with your thoughts and dreams!*

# CHAPTER 1

*Ugh! Nastiest thing in the universe.* I didn't want to touch Thelvienne's body. It resembled a dragon-sized prune rather than the beautiful woman she used to be. My body was still thrumming with energy as I had yet to integrate all of the Queen's magic in with my own.

My heart hadn't settled from Indy 500 levels while my mind analyzed the how's and why's of my magic. Unfortunately, I never figured anything out. And it made me feel like Ron Weasley. Never able to recall spells or the theory behind them.

I went back to wondering why Thelvienne withered like she did. None of the other Fae I'd killed had done that. And the ground was indeed being infected. The ground started sizzling where her blood had splashed. Putrid-smelling smoke drifted into the air while the foliage turned brown around the edges.

"Alright. We'd better get her body through the portal. Pymm's Pondside doesn't deserve to be poisoned by her." I bent and choked as bile rose in my throat.

Aislinn wrinkled her nose. "I love being part of the Backside of Forty, but I think I might draw the line at handling the festering raisin lady."

Bas huffed and lifted the Queen as if she didn't weigh a thing. "I've got her. You'd think you hadn't just killed her or something." He directed the last part at me. Despite the body he was carrying, heat sizzled between us.

I hadn't allowed myself to consider sharing my life with anyone else ever since my husband, Tim, died. He was my first love and always would be. I was happy focusing on my work and my kids until I had my magical new beginning six months ago.

Now, I found myself considering options I could never have even dreamed of. Sebastian was irritable, gruff, and didn't have a romantic bone in his body. But he was also sex walking with muscles on his muscles.

I shook my head at him as I shoved the distracting thoughts away. "I wasn't trying to kill her. Hell, I would have run away screaming if I'd known I was going to absorb her energy. I get the feeling that fact is going to bite me in the ass."

I saw my grams looking out the window above the sink as we passed into the family cemetery on my land. I could see right through her ghostly form to the clock on the wall that told me it was well past midnight. That was why I was exhausted right down to my bones, not because I am a forty-five-year-old hybrid Fae-witch with a bad knee.

A sound rumbled from Bas's chest as he walked beside me. "Is that an invitation? I'd love to bite your delectable bits. But we should be concerned Vodor's anger that his mate was killed."

My body heated, and my mind shut off as I listened to his deep voice. It made me think of nakedness and compromising positions. Heat filled my cheeks, and I spluttered for a response. Sebastian didn't mince words and usually said what was on his mind, so I wasn't certain why his comment had me so flustered.

"You might want to watch it, Bas. She might scald your twig and berries." Aislinn's warning was followed by a round of laughter. The sound of my friends' amusement jolted me and highlighted the reason for my discomfort. Having my friends hear intimate desires made me want to crawl in bed and pull the covers over my head.

Maybe I really was a prude, but I didn't want anyone knowing what Bas wanted to do to me. And I most certainly didn't want anyone knowing how badly I wanted it. Some things were best left to private moments.

I hauled the door to the crypt open and looked back at Aislinn. "Can you hold this open? Once we toss her through, I'm going to take a shower."

"Got it," Aislinn said as she placed a hand on the stone panel.

I walked into the space and looked around at my ancestors' bones that made the foundation of the portal. Lifting my hands, I chanted the spell to open the portal. An oval hovered in the middle of the room, with light surrounding the area. I saw the familiar Fae world of Eidothea through in the center of the oval of light. Seeing a scene of another world in the middle of a crypt where dead people are buried was surreal every time I encountered it.

After the dark Fae had forced the portal open and tried to sneak through to Earth, I was glad it was back to only opening when I gave the mental command. The bright green (almost neon) grass was beautiful, and I could smell the sweet scent of flowers carried on the breeze through the opening.

"Throw the bitch through," I called out to Sebastian over the sound of wind whipping through the small building.

Bas chuckled and approached the portal, then threw what looked like a mummified husk through. I winced when it landed on the grass. It instantly started smoking and turning brown. When the acrid smell started replacing the sweet floral scent, I closed the portal.

Turning, I brushed my hands together and walked out of the mausoleum. "We need to regroup before you guys head home. I desperately need a shower, but I can see grams isn't going to let that happen."

The ghost of my dead grandmother was glaring out the window with her arms crossed over her ample bosom. She wore one of the hideous tops covered in flowers that she loved to wear. The V-neck kept the fabric away from her throat.

I recalled being a little girl and asking her why she wouldn't wear the cute lavender sweater I'd gotten her for her birthday. She told me there was no way in hell she was putting anything on that would constrict around her waddle. She explained that the fabric would choke her, get caught on her chin hairs, and put the extra skin on display.

My hand rose to the skin that was just starting to loosen on my neck. Some days I wish I was that naïve young woman again. When my finger hit something hard and prickly, I lowered my head. I had to at least go to the bathroom and pluck the ugly black hair that had magic all its own.

Seriously, how was it I would rip the little shits out one night, and the next morning, it was back and nearly three inches long?

Bas held the back door open for me. Grams floated in my direction immediately. "What the hell happened out there, Fionna?"

"Not now, Grams. I need to use the restroom." I fled up the stairs and slammed the door the second I entered the bathroom connected to my bedroom. Opening the top drawer, I grabbed the tweezers and thrust my chin toward the mirror.

Gah! I couldn't believe I was fighting the Fae Queen, looking like the bearded lady. My grandmother floated into the room when I was gripping the second hair between the metal.

"You cut me off to pluck your chin hair?" My grams couldn't be louder or sound more irritated.

In my rush to shut her up, I tugged harder than necessary, then lifted my eyes and sent her a glare. "Would you be quiet? I don't need the entire house hearing how I need to shave like a man."

Grams rolled her eyes. "Whatever just happened is going to alert any supernatural across both realms. I want to know what the hell went down out there. I couldn't see anything from the windows."

I yanked the remaining hair out and washed my hands. That's what had her up in arms. I imagined it was difficult for her not to be able to get involved with our battles. Grams had never been shy or one to sit idly by. Part of the reason I was so fierce was that I was her granddaughter.

"I'm sorry about that, but it couldn't be avoided." I opened the door and descended the stairs to the first floor. The house was enormous for a cottage in the countryside. And it was open for being built centuries ago.

The familiar creek of the sixth step and the family pictures on the wall at the base of the stairs helped center and calm me. Everyone was in the kitchen. "You are a Goddess," I praised Violet for making a pot of coffee.

"You never did develop a taste for a proper cuppa." Grams' usual complaint was another comfort. This was why I chose my magical new beginning here in this house. I was surrounded by history and family that helped ground me in any storm. It was also why I fled here right after Tim had died years ago. The three weeks the kids and I spent here helped me face life without Tim.

"You taught me to enjoy tea, but there are times I cannot survive without the blessed dark brew, and this has been a rough night." I inhaled deeply, savoring the roasted coffee bean scent.

Grams had her arms right back over her chest, and one hip cocked to the side. Emotion clogged in my throat with the sight. For longer than I could remember, my grandmother had needed a hip replacement. She'd fallen in her garden and broken it when she was seventy-eight, and it never healed quite right.

To see her sass back as she took her demanding pose was fantastic. "What the hell happened out there? Why did I feel this wave of dark magic ripple through the house? There was no real power behind it, so it made no sense."

I was right back to my childhood and shuffled my feet like I used to when I tried to avoid telling her that I messed up. "Well, remember when I told you about absorbing that Fae's power? I kinda killed the Evil Queen, and her powers floated into me. My blood turned to champagne in my veins. Energy buzzed through me then spread out to Aislinn and Violet," I told her and continued to describe how her body withered, and we tossed her back like she was a fish we didn't want to keep.

Grams' blue-white shape solidified enough that I could no longer see the sofa in the background. "You've landed in another mess, Fiona. Vodor will not let this go. Thelvienne was his life."

The most unladylike snort left me. "I cannot believe she was anything to him but a pain in the ass. They fought constantly, and word on the street was they hated each other."

"Hate and love are often intermixed. I have no doubt he didn't like her, but being with her allowed him to strip creatures of their power. He would never willingly give her up.

His need for her was so great that he overlooked that she was in love with Sebastian and pined for him for centuries. No man in his position would be able to do that if he could live without the woman."

Hearing about Bas's previous girlfriend made my stomach twist into knots. I knew it was ridiculous, but I couldn't change it. I was barely able to hide that fact from my expression.

I glanced in Sebastian's direction and noticed he was scowling at my grams as he sipped from a glass of amber liquid that was no doubt scotch. "I need to check with the council and see if they have any insight."

Camille set her glass in the sink and turned back to the group. "I'll go with you, as well. I'd like to hear what they have to say, too."

In the end, Finarr ended up joining them, which left me, Aislinn, Argies, Violet, and my grams in the kitchen. When the coffee was done burbling and pitting out liquid gold, I poured myself a cup and added plenty of sugar with a splash of cream.

"Do you have any idea how we should handle the King, Grams?"

My grandmother floated to the window over the sink and looked outside. "There is nothing safe for you three to attempt. Vodor has too much power. You might be a *nicotisa,* but you are still learning your craft and what you're capable of. I tried to find as many books and scrolls on the topic as possible, but all there seemed to be were cautionary tales."

"We can't sit around while he kills innocent Fae, Grams. Besides, we won't be facing him alone. Argies and Bas's parents are part of a massive rebellion in Eidothea." I implored her to listen to reason, but she only shook her head which sent her silver hair flying around her shoulders. I looked like waves crashing around her body.

Argies opened his mouth to say something when my internal alarm system pinged me. Groaning, I took another sip of my coffee then set the cup down. "I'll be right back. I'm being paged."

Grams was in front of me instantly and was red around the edges like when she was angry. "You will not go out there, young lady."

My mouth fell open, and I stared at her for several seconds. This was so entirely out of character for her, and I was at a loss for words. My grams was serious about her role as the Portal Guardian. So much so that she set up a spell so I could bring her back from the other side.

At the time, I had no idea how any of it was possible, but I'd learned enough through various conversations that it wasn't merely a matter of having unfinished business. Grams had to cast spells on herself that went soul-deep. That's what I ended up calling back was her spirit.

That was nearly unheard of. The rebellion in Eidothea had been hunting for a way to cast a spell on a soul for centuries. That was the way they felt they would beat Vodor. Their realm was losing its magic and would soon enough be out entirely. No one wanted to think about that possibility.

"Why would you say that to me? I *have* to answer the summons."

Grams had her hands on her ample hips as she narrowed her eyes at me. The look made me feel like I'd disappointed her. It was something I had never handled well. Anytime I got that look, I tripped over myself to make it better.

"You just killed the second most powerful being in the Fae Realm, and you want to go say Hi? I thought I taught you better. You got sucked through last time you tried to repel a dark Fae."

Her words stung, and my mouth immediately wanted to snap, '*You didn't teach me shit. That's why it's been one battle after another since I discovered my magic.'* I bit that sarcastic comment back and took a deep breath.

"You taught me to never shirk my duties. I'm the Portal Guardian now. What if it's someone like Kairi who is being hunted by the king's men? I have to go see who and what it is." I softened my tone, hoping she heard the respect I had for her and her opinion.

Grams' chest heaved as if she was panting, but she made no noise that indicated she even breathed. "I have been doing this a very long time, Fiona. Whoever is trying to get through means us harm. And you would know it if you paid attention to your summons."

"Fair enough. How can I tune into intentions without being face to face?"

Grams lifted her head and smiled at me. "Follow the summons back to its source. You know it's the portal because of experience, but you can trace it back and discover more."

Closing my eyes, I tried to do exactly what she said. Nothing happened, which didn't surprise me at all. The intricacies of performing magic hadn't come naturally to me. Once I figured something out, though, I could cast the spell or access the source with ease, so I tried again. The second I latched onto the trail, energy blasted through it and slammed into me.

I felt my body fly through the air at the same time dark energy scalded my veins. It hurt like a bitch and made me cry out. My eyes snapped open, and I saw the island pass below me. My heart struggled to beat, and my lungs wanted to shut down. Before my mind could catch up with what was happening, my back hit a corner, and a loud crack filled the room.

Argies was somehow in front of me and catching me before I hit the wood floor. Tears streamed down my face as

I tried my hardest to suck in a breath. My lungs felt like deflated balloons in my chest.

Grams was in front of me, and Aislinn and Violet were shouting something. Argies carried me from the kitchen and to the living room. I cried out with every step he took. "I'm sorry, Fiona. Hang in there until I can set you on the couch."

"She's bluer than you are, Isidora. What do we do?" That was Violet's frantic voice.

"Join hands and cast a spell to force her Fae side ascendant. It will heal her lungs before she dies."

I heard my friends shout, *"Ascendant Fae."* Warmth surrounded me at the same time Argies set me on the soft cushion. It caused a sharp pain to slice through my chest. I swear my heart stopped for several seconds.

Thankfully, after that, the pain lessened enough, and I could take in small gasps of air. Violet and Aislinn knelt in front of me with Argies and Grams behind them. It took an eternity for me to suck in a full breath. The pain was horrendous, but it no longer threatened to make me blackout.

"What…the…hell…was that?"

Grams had a frown on her face. "It was a trap like I was worried about. Vodor is powerful indeed if he was able to hit you through a source, he shouldn't even be able to access."

Sweat covered my body, and nausea churned in my stomach while the pain receded at a snail's pace. I was entirely too old for this crap. And unprepared for this magical twist. Even if I wanted to go back on my promise to help fight Vodor, it wasn't possible now.

He could reach me without ever leaving Eidothea. Guilt rose to join the party of nausea, agony, and bile. He was likely making innocent Fae pay for me killing the Queen as I laid there struggling to stay alive.

"I'm sorry for questioning you, Grams. I don't think I would have survived if I'd gone into the crypt."

"You might not survive the night. He managed to take out most of the protections on Pymm's Pondside that have been built by countless generations of Shakletons."

I sat up so fast I couldn't even stop myself. Black spots danced in my vision, and I lost my battle with bile, throwing up all over my lap. A decade later, after the heaving died down, I wiped my mouth with the back of my hand.

"Looks like we need to rebuild those first. I'll just need a minute." Or a year. That would work much better, but I didn't think the Evil King would allow me the opportunity.

## CHAPTER 2

I sat up with a groan and rubbed my head. What the hell had woken me up? A tiny man was slamming a hammer against the inside of my skull. I couldn't form a coherent thought. "Agh!" Blinking was an exercise in painful sandpaper scrubbing my cornea raw.

*What time is it?* It felt like I just barely laid down. Groping around the side table next to my bed, I shoved my cell to the floor. Shouting outside prompted me to get my ass in gear. I'd like to think I jumped right out of bed, but really, I lumbered and picked up my phone to see it was barely four-thirty in the morning.

My chest ached, reminding me I hadn't healed from the attack a few hours ago. I should be laid up in a hospital somewhere, resting and allowing the broken ribs the time needed to be able to breathe easily again. I shouldn't be up and about already, and my chest was screaming at me to get back in bed. That wasn't going to be possible until I discovered what was causing the commotion. The last thing I wanted was to have my home infiltrated by dark Fae while I laid around in bed.

I opened my connection to Pymm's Pondside and tried to see if I could feel an incursion. I hadn't been able to replace all of the protections last night. I had given up, figuring Vodor must have been spent after using so much power to attack me through the portal.

Snatching my robe from its hanger on the back of my door, I threw it on as I ran down the stairs. "Grams!" My shout echoed throughout the spacious house. I never knew where she spent her time, so yelling for her was usually my way of locating her.

A door to my left opened, and a bleary-eyed Violet stood there pushing her hair off her face. "What's happening?"

"Not sure," I replied. My grandmother floated through a wall to my right as I descended the stairs. "Do you know who's yelling outside?"

Grams glared at me, which was disconcerting, to say the least. She was semitransparent, and I could see a framed picture of my kids at Disneyland behind her. "I have no idea. I can't leave the house, Fiona."

"I haven't forgotten, Grams. I figured you were connected to everything here." I winced when I heard another door opening, knowing I had woken Aislinn, as well. Neither of my best friends had wanted to leave me alone last night with me being so vulnerable, and Bas hadn't returned when we headed for bed.

"Why are we up so early?" Aislinn's voice was raspy and far more sleepy than Violet or I had been. She should be able to spring up like a daisy. She was the youngest of the three of us, turning forty in a few months.

"Something is happening outside." Violet responded since I was already halfway down the stairs.

I missed a step at the bottom when pain lanced through my chest. Sucking in a breath, I caught myself on the wall and rubbed the spot. Thankfully it seemed to vanish. Continuing to the mudroom, I shoved my feet into my rain boots and went outside.

The smell of a campfire hit me first. I stood there while Violet and Aislinn joined me and scanned the area. There were no signs of flames or anything of that nature. The pond was placid, and the forest surrounding the house was serene.

"What do we do? I can call the water over here." That was Kairi's voice.

Heart in my throat, I ran toward the left, figuring she was in the cemetery. When we cleared the side of the house, I finally found the source of the smoke. I saw Kairi, Theamise, and Tunsall standing outside the mausoleum while it was engulfed in dark blue flames. Adrenalin and fear kicked me into gear.

It was better than a quad shot espresso. My heart dropped back to my chest and went into v-tach, and the world swam around me for several seconds while I made my way to their side.

I stopped next to the mermaid and had to brace myself on my knees while I caught my breath. "If you really can bring the water from the pond to put this out, do it right now."

My heart constricted painfully, and I knew I was in v-tach. It wasn't just a racing heart. It felt like it wasn't filling with blood and was threatening to give out. The agony was back, and it dropped me to my knees, making my bad one scream at me. *For once, you aren't my biggest pain.*

"Fiona! What in creation is going on out there." I heard my Grams' voice yelling out at me, but I couldn't respond.

Violet and Aislinn knelt next to me. "Are you alright?" Both women bombarded me with the same question.

"Not sure. Can you guys help me up?"

Rather than respond, they each threaded an arm under one of mine and tugged. I poured what energy I could into getting upright and finally managed. But not before those pesky black dots were back and trying to take me under again.

I fought it back, and by the time my vision cleared, I could see a beautiful arch of crystal-clear water flying overhead and pouring over the crypt where the portal was housed. That was the noise I heard. It hadn't just been the blood rushing through my body as it tried to resume normal flow.

"It's not working," Kairi called out.

I looked from the flames to the mermaid and noticed the strain on her pinched face. She had her hands held aloft while sweat beaded on her brow. "Crap. It must be a magical fire. You can drop the water. I don't want you to hurt yourself."

Turning around, I was grateful my friends had a hold of my arms when I nearly collapsed. "Grams! How do you fight a Fae fire? I think the king is burning the portal and crypt down."

"That's not possible. He has no power over what our family created. It's outside his ability." I could see her hovering in the kitchen window that looked out over the garden to the cemetery.

Beside me, Aislinn stumbled and fell into my side. Violet ended up taking the brunt of our weight for a few seconds until we both steadied. It wasn't easy. The pain was getting worse, and my lungs were threatening to go along with my heart.

"Somehow the...asshole figured... out away." It was getting difficult to breathe.

"Is the structure going? Or are the flames on top of it?" I wasn't sure that it mattered or why Grams thought that was important. I also couldn't answer.

"The stone is on fire, but it isn't actually burning. It's turning to ash, I think. It's hard to see through the dark fire."

Theamise shifted from foot to foot as she told Grams what was happening. The slender wood nymph was a gentle creature and didn't deal well with strife, unlike the tiny brownie standing next to her, twisting her red dress in her hands.

"Did you do something, Tunsall?" I growled the question as my anger ignited and overrode some of the pain.

Tunstall's large green eyes flipped up in my direction, and I could see the tears shining in them. "I didn't do anything, Fiona. I promise. I would never go against you or your family again. You gave me a second chance, and I wouldn't do anything to jeopardize that. Besides, my sister was killed, so there isn't much they can hold over me to force me into action anymore. I know they won't abide by their promises anyway."

I believed the brownie. I'd seen her grief firsthand. And she had helped me during my first battle with the dead Queen, so she'd chosen her side. My body swayed as the anger receded, taking my energy with it. Violet tried to hold all three of us up, but my chest constricted, and my legs gave out.

"What's wrong, Fiona?" Grams sounded far closer than inside the house.

"It feels like I'm on fire, and my organs are shutting down, I think." The words left me in a whisper. Every inch of skin on my body felt raw, like I'd stepped into the flames and stood there for several seconds. It was a hot flash that seared my flesh to my bones and involved unending agony. Violet ended up relaying what I said to Grams while Aislinn knelt next to me, cradling my head.

"Fiona, you need to cut your connection to the portal. Vodor is using it to kill you." A sinister laugh seemed to float on the air with Grams' command.

*Cut my connection?* I tried to find the thread and found nothing but agony. My head was a mess, and all I knew was agony. I no longer felt the cool breeze. All I heard was the crackle of a fire, and my nose was filled with charred flesh. That got my attention.

"Did anyone go inside the crypt?" My words were mostly breath, but my friends heard me.

Tunsall laid a small palm on my overheated cheek. "No one is inside. I think Vodor is sacrificing the Gods know how many on his side to fuel this spell." That made me gag. How could the guy be so evil? It was a stupid question, but I couldn't help wondering why people were willing to harm others to gain power.

Aislinn jerked and moaned, drawing my attention. She seemed to be affected by this too. "How do you feel, Violet?"

"What is going on? Did you cut your connection, Fiona?" I couldn't answer Grams. I needed to know if this was hurting my friends, as well.

Fiona glanced down at me, and I could see the lines deepen in her face. "I feel like I've been run over by a truck, and the hot flashes won't stop, but I'll be okay."

I looked at Aislinn and swallowed the lump in my throat. Sometimes being stubborn helped. My determination made it easier to talk through constricted lungs. "He is attacking both of you through your connection to me. You guys should cut it off and save yourselves."

"No," Violet snapped.

"Not happening. If we can share this, maybe you can find a way to beat him back," Aislinn added.

I couldn't ask for better friends. They were the freakin best to have at my side. I knew they had their own midlife reboot, but I hadn't been able to help them like I wanted. We'd been too focused on one crisis after another. I would be there for them, whatever they needed as soon as we dealt with Vodor.

"Fiona!" Sebastian's voice was a balm to my scorched

skin. I could see him, Finarr, and Argies running to us over Aislinn's shoulder. Within seconds he was there and scooping me up into his arms. Argies grabbed hold of Aislinn.

I braced myself for the agony to follow and was surprised when I was able to suck in a breath, and my heart filled with blood again. I was still in pain, but it was less now. "Let go of me."

Bas's head jerked, and his face crumpled. For a split second, before he masked his emotions, I saw the hurt cross his features. Before I could explain, he let go of me, and the agony was back full force.

I reached for him and wrapped my arms around him. Once again, the pain lessened. "Somehow you take away some of the misery. I just wanted to test a theory. Please don't let me go until I can work through this mess."

Sebastian's gaze filled with too many emotions for me to decipher. "Always. I'm sorry it took me so long. We came as soon as we felt the dark fire."

"Thank you for always having my back. I'd say you can join the Backside of Forty with us, but it's a women's only club."

Bas chuckled and shook his head, then placed a quick kiss on my lips. I wanted more and was about to go for more when my grandmother's voice interrupted us. "Now is not the time for kissing, Fiona. Cut your connection, now! It's killing you."

"I can't sever the tie, Grams. If I do, I am giving control over to Vodor, and I will never do that." Now that I was able to think a bit, I realized what he was trying to do.

"Shit." I glanced at the window where my Grams was hovering inside the house. I saw the way she wrung what looked like a doily while she paced a short circuit.

"How do we stop this?" Violet asked.

"I'm going to try and contain it. If I can manage that, maybe I can find a permanent solution. Let's move away a few feet."

Sebastian helped me limp a few steps. I was glad to see Violet and Aislinn walking independently. However, Argies remained close to them both with his eyes trained on Aislinn.

Finnair, Theamise, Tunsall, and Kairi joined us, and I closed my eyes then searched for my connection to the elements. I usually felt energy flow inside me like a river. Now it more closely resembled a dry creek bed.

Grabbing hold of everything I could in that flow, I chanted, "*Quae.*"

Energy immediately flooded through my funnel. I allowed my rage over Vodor's hubris and cruelty to fuel my spell until my fingers tingled. I hadn't had to try so hard to access my magic for the past four or five months. And even in the beginning, I never had to focus so intently on accessing the well and wielding it. It happened accidentally.

There was no way in hell I was giving anything to this asshole. He wouldn't take that much from me. Opening my eyes, I saw the shimmer that represented my magic grow in a giant dome over the now crumbling crypt.

The pain nearly disappeared the second the dark magic was enclosed inside my cocoon. The second it snapped into place, I heard both Aislinn and Violet heave a sigh of relief. Turning, I checked to see their complexion was no longer quite so green around the gills.

"You cut him off from the source," Grams called out in a louder voice and drawing my attention to her. The fire must have been making more noise than I realized. That and I could no longer hear my heart pounding in my ears.

Turning around, I saw that she'd managed to get the window open somehow. "The flames are below the roofline but not out. Do you have any idea how he is doing any of this? Did you find any of our ancestors that might have information to share?"

"I spoke with my mother, and she said that you definitely weakened him when you killed his wife, but I don't think she was right. Unless grandma Eunice was right, and he knows what you are and is scrambling to steal your power from you."

I was betting my great-great-grandma Eunice was right. I felt him draining the life from me. I saw the result of my river drying up. "I don't think that helps us one bit."

"The flames are gone!"

My head swiveled around when I heard Violet's excited voice. I swear I gave myself whiplash. My jaw dropped when I saw she was right. The dark fire was gone, leaving a charred mess in its wake. The roof was gone entirely and three-quarters of the front wall along with it. The other three walls were half of their usual height.

Tears welled in my eyes that someone had desecrated my ancestors in such a way—a lump formed in my throat next. The king had stolen something from me. The crypt was a symbol of my magical new beginning, and now he'd ruined it.

I blinked to clear the blur from my vision, and a gasp escaped me. The tombstones and remains of the mausoleum were aging before my eyes. It was as if the magic was being sucked from the sacred land.

The first time I'd seen an old cemetery in the States, I was surprised that the names on the headstones were barely legible. The ones here in my family's place of rest remained as pristine as the day they'd been made, until now.

"No!" The denial flew from my mouth, and I rushed to great-great-grandma Eunice's grave. My steps slowed when I hit the barrier I'd erected.

Pushing through felt like trying to swim through a pool of pudding. Once I made it to the other side, my energy evaporated, and the pain was back. And not only that, my body reverted to what it had been before all this running around. Every ache and pain had returned with a vengeance.

Sebastian had told me once he thought I would stop aging and maybe even regain some of my youthful vigor after my powers were unlocked. I'd dismissed the idea out of hand. Now I realized he'd been right, and it had been happening subtly.

I still had the body of a middle-aged woman, but it was in far better shape now. My legs gave out on me once again, and I caught myself on a headstone. The rock crumbled beneath my hand.

My heart went into v-tach again, the lower chambers not filling entirely with blood while it raced far too fast. I needed to get the hell out of this shield. Vodor was taking every last ounce of magic he could from my family's land. Pretty soon, there would be nothing left of Pymm's Pondside.

Strong arms banded around me, allowing my heart to fill and my pain to recede. Sebastian. "I've got you, love. You can't cross your spell until you figure out how to stop Vodor."

Nodding, I allowed him to help me cross to the other side where Vodor couldn't reach me. Violet was chewing on her lower lip while Aislinn had her arms around her middle and was clutching her sides.

The vice around my chest eased, and I stood straight again. "He is definitely stealing magic. And he zeros in on me when he can feel me close."

Violet released her abused lip and snorted. "That's because you're a lightning rod full of power."

I chuckled, appreciating the levity. It reminded me that life was about more than fighting this evil despite the chaos of the past few days. My steps continued toward the backdoor and my Grams. My friends fell into step, and Sebastian stuck close to my side.

"The King is trying to destroy what he sees as the seat of your power, the portal. He doesn't realize there is far more to you than that and likely doesn't care. He wants to cut you off at the knees." Finarr's observation turned my blood to ice and made Bas growl low in his throat.

Finarr clearly dismissed the idea of the portal as feeding my power, but what if he was wrong? It would be just my luck for the king to cut me off and weaken me significantly while also denying us the chance to return and help overthrow him. It kinda made sense.

Grams said I shouldn't be affected by the destruction, yet I was. Was this going to stop me? No freakin way. I'd never let anything stop me, and I wasn't about to start now.

# CHAPTER 3

"This isn't good." I wanted to say, '*No shit, Sherlock. What was your first clue?*' But Grams wouldn't appreciate the sass. Besides, I imagined she was still processing what was happening. "I think mom and grandma were onto something but didn't really hit the mark with their theories. I'd bet my afterlife Vodor is trying to reclaim his mate's power. I doubt he understands that you absorbed it."

My eyes flew wide as I toed off my boots and cradled my side. "Holy crap. I think you're right. If he was aware of me and targeting me specifically for my power, he wouldn't be stealing it from everywhere. The flames were directed at me for sure."

"He likely used the commotion to seed his spell before we could stop him," Aislinn added.

Violet grabbed the teapot and filled it with water while everyone gathered in the kitchen. "We need to find a way to stop him from sucking Pymm's Pondside dry."

"Is that even possible? I have his enchantment contained. Perhaps I can keep it to those three-square feet." It sounded ridiculous the moment I said it. Not that it wasn't a valid question.

Grams shook her disheveled silver hair. How the heck did a ghost's hair, get tangled anyway? She was incorporeal, so it shouldn't be possible. "Eventually he will sink feelers into the soil and spread it out. Now that he has a taste for how much power our land contains, he won't stop until he has it all."

"We need to stop him before that happens," Sebastian cut in.

"Do you have any idea how we do that?" I needed to grab some of the books upstairs, but I would take them if he had any ideas. I hated feeling helpless.

Bas shook his head from side to side as he leaned against the doorframe. "The only thing that comes to mind is for us to get to what remains of the mausoleum and have you open the crippled portal and pray we aren't sent to another realm, then hunt him down and kill him."

"We don't have that kind of time." Grams' voice faded as she was speaking. My heart leaped painfully in my chest. The poor organ had been through so much. My entire body had been battered relentlessly over the past twenty-four hours.

I wanted to wail like a three-year-old about the unfairness of life. I might be losing my Grams and my magic, and all I could think about was crawling in bed and taking a nap.

"Can you sense him stripping the land of power, now?" The bluish image of Grams flickered even as I asked. He had to be stealing some of the power that enabled her to remain with me.

Grams tilted her head and went motionless. I jumped toward her, but my hand went right through her. My skin chilled as it passed and made me shiver. I waited several seconds, my heart racing and breathing increased as my grams remained frozen.

"I have to try something." I was at the backdoor and

heading out without shoes on. Several footsteps pounded behind me, letting me know my friends had followed just like I expected.

I paused at the edge of my cocoon and lifted my hands. "*Saeclum*." When my bubble started to unravel, I recast the spell and held my breath until hundreds of tiny holes hit my shield instead. He had booby-trapped his enchantment.

Looking to Bas, I told him I needed to go inside the bubble. That was the only way to ensure my enchantment was directed at the right source. He grabbed my hand, grounding me before I crossed. Moving through the thick layer was far easier than the last time.

My entire body felt like it was being drained while my ears were stuffed with cotton. It reminded me of being on an airplane or in a hyperbaric chamber with a patient. Once pressurized, your ears felt like they needed to pop, and everything sounded far away. There was also a draw on my chest as my energy was being hoovered by the evil Fae King.

Squeezing Sebastian's hand, I muttered my spell to disband Vodor's. For a second, I thought it was going to work. The walls of the crypt flickered, and I saw the bones reform up above the existing stone structure. Unfortunately, it didn't continue.

The blowback when the spell was smashed made my hair fly back behind me. If not for Sebastian, I would have ended up on my ass. "You have any other ideas?"

Bas pursed his lips and moved behind me, then wrapped his arms around me. I loved the sensation and wanted to melt into him. Unfortunately, we had an asshole to cut off. When I was about to let him know that very pertinent fact, he shared his idea with me. "Let's combine our power. That might be enough to stop his progress. I think you're onto the right idea, but you need more support."

I shrugged my shoulders, trying to hide the way the mere

idea made my insides turn all warm and squishy. I wanted to get closer to him. We'd fooled around, and I thought I was finally ready to take it even further. Later. When Vodor had been dealt with.

"Sounds good to me." Both of us chanted the spell again, and I watched as even more of my ancestors' remains returned. It didn't last, though. One thing was clear, stopping him would bring back the bones that lined the crypt walls, but it wouldn't remake the actual surrounding structure. I had known the power of the portal was in the skeletons. This was further confirmation.

"Try to cast a dissipation spell." Violet's voice was warbled as it passed through my cocoon to reach us.

I liked the idea, while at the same time, I was unsure if it was a good idea. I tried to think the problem through, but my energy dwindled rapidly. I felt suffocated and couldn't catch my breath.

I refused to send Vodor's magic to the town. The ocean wasn't far from our current location. Dispersing it in that direction meant endangering everything in its path. Aislinn lived on the cliffs along with countless humans and supernaturals alike. It would be like deliberately dumping toxic waste in the water or burying it beneath the soil.

The rot would eventually eat away at the nutrients, slowly poisoning everything it came into contact with. Once he established a foothold in enough places, he would have an endless supply of power, and he wouldn't have to destroy Eidothea as he took it. No. Spreading his filth around wasn't going to work for me.

"That's too risky. And would give his little suckers others to latch onto and suck dry. There has to be something we can do." Fatigue was making me short-tempered. "I can't stay in here anymore. I need to get out so I can think straight."

Bas shifted his hold and twined our fingers together as

we headed to the group. I continued until we reached the house. I had to check and see if Grams was still frozen. My heart fell to my feet when I saw Grams frozen in a new spot. It looked like she'd been heading to the window when she went immobile again.

I turned away from the house and rubbed my sore ribs while watching the progress I had made slowly disintegrate once again. "Dissipation isn't an option, and I'm not strong enough to dissolve the spell altogether. Anyone have any other ideas? Or which book should I start looking in?"

"What if you feed your connection to the elements?" Aislinn was hesitant, and I knew she was grasping, but I didn't cut her off. I owed it to her to listen. She and Violet had been there for me and supported every one of my efforts.

"I can help rejuvenate your connection to the water," Kairi added, making me gasp. I hadn't seen the mermaid leaning on her elbows at the side of the pond.

Theamise was off to the side with Tunsall. The wood nymph's head was bobbing up and down. "And I can help you bond with the earth."

I had no idea if the plan would actually work, but it was our best bet. I looked at each of my friends in turn, and each of them nodded in agreement. "Let's do it. You should know that the connection is still there. It's just smothered, for lack of a better description."

I approached the pond and paused when I was a couple feet away. With a groan, I knelt on the ground, so I was closest to Kairi. "What should I do now?"

"It'll work best if you join me in the water."

Of course, it would. I was covered in ash and needed a shower. It would have been so much better to stand under a stream hot enough to wash everything away. Especially if Bas joined me. *No. Bad Fiona. It's not sexy time.*

My friends were a steady presence behind me as I removed the robe, handing it to Aislinn, then plopped onto my butt and swung my leg into the water. "I doubt I have enough energy to tread water for very long. Promise you won't let me drown."

Kairi giggled at that. "I would never let that happen."

Good enough for me. Pushing off with my palms, I tried to arch my body into the water. What I intended to be a graceful move ended up making me look like a torpedoed whale. My chest and abs protested every movement, and my stiff body flopped with a big splash.

My head was engulfed by cool water. I ran my hands over my hair and face, trying to wash away some of the grime. I sucked in a breath when I surfaced a second later. Violet and Aislinn were peering into the water while Bas, Finarr, and Argies watched.

"That looks refreshing," Violet said as she pulled her shirt away from her body. I saw the telltale sweat dotting her upper lip and forehead.

"It feels fantastic," I told her before turning to the mermaid. "Okay, now what?"

Kairi grabbed my hands and closed her eyes. I watched as a subtle glow started under her skin. It spread to the water. Before long, the entire pond glowed blue. The lily pads on top seemed to plump and rejuvenate.

My legs were tired before entering the water, and now they were limp noodles. It was nearly impossible to keep my head above the surface without using my hands. I could likely stop moving altogether, and Kairi would make sure I didn't sink to the bottom.

Instinct refused to let my legs take a break. Kairi was now a mermaid-shaped glowstick, and the water tingled as it surrounded me. It helped invigorate my legs and keep me moving. Within seconds my blood thinned and seemed to crash in waves against the walls of my veins. I couldn't describe the sensation any other way.

My blood volume increased, making me feel like it was swaying back and forth far less. The wind picked up and blew cool air across my face. The combination was electric. A quick check of my dry creek bed, and I was shocked to find it was much fuller now.

Kairi continued sending energy my way for several more seconds before a wave lifted me out of the water and set me on my feet next to Violet. "Your skin is glowing. Not as much as Kairi's, but there's a distinct blue glow."

I lifted an arm when Violet spoke and poked my forearm. She was right. I look like a Glo Worm. "That was the best idea all night. My river is a third full again, and I have more energy. Let's do the earth too. Then I can face that asshole again."

Aislinn and Violet chuckled while Sebastian looked at me with narrowed eyes. I sensed his muscles jumping as he held himself back. He didn't like the idea of me facing Vodor. He'd better get used to it. I was in this fight whether I wanted it or not.

Theamise stepped forward with a broad smile on her face. "Let's go to the garden. Tunsall and the pixies will join us, so your access is greater. None of us are of the royal line like Kairi."

I wrung my hair out as we walked and tried to do the same with my t-shirt. I was tempted to remove the thing and put on my dry robe, but I wasn't wearing a bra. Allowing Bas to see me naked was one thing. There was no way I wanted anyone else to see what I looked like without clothes. My body was a roadmap of scars, stretch marks, and loose skin.

I wasn't nervous about Bas seeing my imperfections. He looked at me as if he was dying of thirst, and only I could quench it. No one aside from him had ever looked at me with such intense desire. Just thinking about it made me shiver.

The still bluish image of my Grams distracted that thought as we passed the window. She'd managed to move closer before freezing again. I followed Theamise to a bay tree placed near some angelica. There we stopped, and my friends circled us. Kairi had joined them this time.

Theamise grabbed one of my hands. "Take Tunsall's hand. We need to form a circle."

Bobbing my head, I knelt on one knee, so I was touching the brownie. A pixie took her hand, and Theamise closed the circle by connecting with the last pixie. I was immediately surrounded by the smell of fresh flowers and herbs. I could feel the dirt under my feet and the life of the plants all around us.

The physical link enabled me to feel the shift of the soil and the worms beneath the surface. They all closed their eyes. The pixies' wings never stopped the hummingbird-fast pace of their beating. Like it had with Kairi, a subtle glow started under Theamise's skin. I noticed the same with Tunsall and the pixies.

Theamise's inner light was brown while Tunsall's was darker, and the pixies were all different colors. One was pink, one was green, and another was teal. The light spread from our feet to the ground. Before long, the entire garden glowed brightly.

The strength returned to my body, and the pain in my ribs even decreased. I soaked in the energy like a sponge, and I felt every grain of sand and leaves on the trees. We were surrounded by so much life. Thanks to my cocoon, none of the vile energy had infiltrated the rest of Pymm's Pondside.

We looked like a fairy ring. I kinda wish I had a drone so I could see what we looked like from the sky. The ground and air tingled all around us. It was like a boost of caffeine. My blood sang with vigor and nearly brought me back to normal. I had no doubt my river would run dry the second I crossed my bubble, but I was relieved the drain wasn't permanent.

The wind picked up and nearly froze me. I was dripping wet and wanted to head inside but didn't move as I enjoyed leaves rustling all around us. My river was over two-thirds full now, and I conjured a fireball to my hand with relative ease.

"Looks like it worked," Bas said, breaking the silence. Theamise dropped my hand with a smile.

"Thank you, guys. I'm not sure I would have realized what I needed to do to stop Vodor or been able to do it, for that matter. I was dangerously close to burning out."

"What do we need to do?" Violet asked while Aislinn blurted, "How the heck did you figure it out while getting an energy injection?"

I laughed and held up a hand. "That sounded vile, Ais. It was the method of how they helped reinforce my connection to the elements that made me realize how I could get enough power to dissolve Vodor's spell. My family created the portal and have been its Guardian for centuries. I can't push Vodor back without Grams' help. The problem is too damn big. I need to bond physically with Grams." I was already heading to the back door while I spoke.

Relief slammed into me when I saw Grams was no longer frozen. She was still faint around the edges but able to interact once more. I raced up the stairs to the attic, explaining to Grams what I need to do.

When I paused inside the workroom, I glanced at my friends, who had been awfully quiet since my proclamation outside. Finarr and Argies looked at me with their jaws on their chests. Aislinn and Violet simply nodded. Bas looked hurt and proud at the same time. I know he wanted me to need him. And I did. Just not for his power. I needed him to ground me and keep the dark energy at bay.

"Try the family grimoire," Grams told me, kicking me back into gear. I grabbed the hefty tome and started flipping through the pages. I gave up hope of there being anything in there to help me when I came across a spell to allow a connection to the dead.

"I've got it! There's a spell here to bond a spirit with their physical body. Looks simple enough."

This was the break we'd been needing. A weight lifted from my shoulders as I turned to grab the ingredients I would need. *Watch out motherfucker. You'll regret messing with a Shakleton.*

# CHAPTER 4

"You cannot do it." I gaped at Grams when her vehement words spilled from her ghostly form. How did she talk anyway? I'd wondered it a hundred times and was thinking about it right now because I couldn't think about the hurt that pierced my chest with her statement.

She didn't believe I could do it. It was surprisingly awful to hear her lack of faith in my abilities. I'd always wanted to make her proud, even more so now that I'd discovered what I really was.

"I know you don't believe in me, but there's no choice, Grams." I sounded like a petulant child even to my own ears.

"Fiona, it is magic that is far beyond your experience, and while the ingredients appear to be straightforward, there is nothing easy about this kind of spell. Messing with the dead, their souls, and bodies is advanced magic. You'd be delving into necromancy. That can turn a witch dark if they aren't careful."

I stormed to the window set in the attic's front, turned workspace, and pointed to the cemetery below. "Our ancestors are being destroyed. Vodor is stealing the energy from us. I have no idea how he found a flaw in the portal, let alone a spell to exploit said fault, but he did. And he is now stealing power from us. You were frozen just a moment ago."

Grams stopped a couple feet away from the window, and her image flickered like a faulty signal on a television. "I don't want to lose you. What would Emmie, Skylar, and Greyson do without their mother?" Pulling my kids into the argument was a low blow. She was well aware I worked hard to ensure they knew they were loved and cared for.

To my surprise, Sebastian stepped up to us. "That was unnecessary, Isidora. Hurting Fiona to get what you want isn't going to change her mind. She's selfless to a fault. She is always willing to jump into a problem with both feet without letting her fear or the risk to herself stop her. There would be far more killed in Cottlehill Wilds without her bravery. She will do what needs to be done to ensure your family doesn't lose everything and the portal survives."

Emotion clogged my throat for the hundredth time that night. I swear menopause sometimes sucked with the massive hormone fluctuations. I went from bawling to screaming in no time. Alright, so most of it was the bullshit Vodor and Thelvienne kept putting me through, but still.

"I would like your help, Grams. I refuse to let the legacy you passed down to me be decimated by that vile Fae."

Grams sighed, her chest rising and falling and the sound leaving her mouth all without me feeling her breath on my face. She was close enough, and her exhalation deep enough it should have blown the hair framing my face. "Alright. Grab the big cauldron."

I wanted to hug her but couldn't, so I crossed to the bookshelves and picked up the large black spot on the bottom shelf. It looked exactly like the pictures showed. Rounded bottom with a lip on top and two horseshoe-shaped handles on the sides. It was also heavier than I anticipated, and I had to grab the holds with two hands. Along with the object's weight, I couldn't stop the apprehension that shivered through my chest. The last thing I wanted was to turn dark. I didn't even know what that meant.

My side protested the exertion, distracting me from my worries, and I nearly dropped the black, iron pot. Violet was there, helping me lift it to the table. "Do we need to use heat?" I didn't see anywhere to create a fire in the attic and wondered if that was done downstairs. The few potions I had made with Camille had been in the smaller cauldrons, and we'd used a pot to contain the flames beneath it.

Grams bobbed her head. "Yes. I use magic to spell a fireplace in the corner there," she pointed to an empty space in the far right of the attic away from the door. When I looked closer, I could see the black char marks on the floor.

"I hadn't noticed that before. Now I can feel magic humming in that section. It's different than the rest of the house. I think I can sense the protective structure that has been cast there for hundreds of years."

Grams tilted her head and stared at me. Perhaps she was frozen again and continued to feel out the energy and then cast my spell. I kept in mind the stone fireplace and chimney as I muttered the incantation I thought would produce the enchantment.

Everyone in the room gasped, including my grandmother. "What?" I asked as I set the cauldron on the tripod I added, then turned back to the room.

"You shouldn't have been able to feel a structure there. Our spells were merely protective, so we didn't burn down the house." Grams' explanation was cut off by Violet.

"You actually created a fireplace, complete with a chimney. I've only been able to manage simple construction tasks, and I always had to have the supplies on hand to do them," Violet added.

"What? Are you saying this is real? That it will stay here? All I did was think about the stone of the house and how they built the fireplace downstairs with it." My heart was racing, and my breathing was bordering on hyperventilating.

Aislinn tapped the family grimoire. "We can discuss how Fiona's power is getting stronger later. We have a potion to make."

I nodded my head. "You're right. Let's get to work." Violet and Aislinn helped me with the potion. Aislinn raced to the garden and grabbed some fresh garlic and cilantro. Violet started the fire, and I added energy to the flames. Before long, the pot was full and bubbling. It was also the same bluish color as Grams. The potency of the herbs mixing together made my head swim, and my stomach churned.

I used to think you could always use garlic in any given recipe. Now I wasn't so sure. The odor wasn't rancid but was strong as hell. Needing to get the heck out of the small room, I directed Grams to a spot, then I cast a circle of salt around her, calling on the elements.

Once the circle was done, I lifted my arms and, using telekinetic powers, made it stream from the pot to hover over Grams. "*Vinculo animus corpori.*"

Thunder and lightning echoed throughout the attic right before a monsoon started. I let go of the potion, so it flowed over Grams. It coated her ghostly shape, and the second the liquid hit the floor, she was sucked away by some unseen force. A scream left my mouth. Oh no. I messed up the spell, and now I'd lost my Grams forever. I'd been so worried about going dark that I hadn't listened to the rest of what Grams said. That I wasn't ready.

My heart shattered in my chest. I'd lost her all over again. I was tired of losing people I loved. There was only so much grief anyone could handle, and I wasn't sure I'd come out intact this time. Because this time, I lost Grams because of my hubris. It was my fault she was gone.

Sebastian raced from the room. I didn't blame him for wanting to get away from me. I was a black widow. I braced myself on the table and tried to suck in a full breath, but I couldn't manage to fill my lungs.

Pounding footsteps had me jerking my head up. Had he come back? No. What was left of my heart disintegrated. At least that's how it felt. Everyone had left me in the attic. I heard the door slam a second later, confirming they were running from me.

The wind stopped suddenly, so did the monsoon rains. The attic remained dry, along with the books and vials on their shelves. Nothing was even wet. That is if you didn't count me because I was drenched from head to toe.

With the noise of the wind and rains gone, I heard a commotion outside. Rushing to the window, I couldn't comprehend what I was seeing. Violet and Aislinn were dripping water into the dirt while they stood there and watched Argies and Bas digging into the soil. They were far too close to the bubble for my comfort.

I ran downstairs and outside. I barely remember flying through the house before I was standing next to my friends. Finarr had joined Argies and Sebastian in digging. Sand flew out behind them in handfuls. I opened my mouth to apologize for failing when they stopped.

My skin prickled with energy. Thinking it was Vodor and that he'd managed to get past my spell, I glanced up to see the shimmer of my veil still in place. My heart was beating faster than a hummingbird's wings, and my chest was on fire once again. The broken ribs hadn't healed enough for me to be running around like I was.

When I looked back down, I blinked in shock. "What the

fuck?" I hadn't meant to curse. It wasn't something I did very often, but the expletive fit the situation. Finarr and Argies were pulling Grams out of the ground.

My gaze shifted to the marble stone, and it was at that moment I realized we were standing on top of Grams' grave. Why were they digging her up? Her head lolled forward on her chest, and her silver hair was matted with dirt.

Sebastian set the lid off the wooden coffin and watched as the dragon and the elf wrapped an arm around her waist. I screamed louder than before when she lifted her head and blinked her green eyes at me.

I had been shocked at how good she looked during her wake and was doubly shocked now. I knew all too well how a body decomposes, but it looked like Grams hadn't decayed much. Sure, her skin could use a thick layer of lotion, but that was pretty much it.

And I hadn't had her embalmed either. She had taught me from an early age that Shakleton's didn't do that. I never understood why before seeing the crypt. If I pumped her body full of chemicals, it might strip the magic from her bones. And the bones and blood helped fortify our land.

My spell had shoved her back inside her body. Without thinking, I wrapped my arms around her midsection and started sobbing. "I can't believe that worked." Pulling back, I felt my cheeks heat as I looked up at my grandmother, who had begun tsking me.

"You can let go of me now." All three of us released her, and she stumbled before righting herself. How were her muscles working at all? I wanted to hug her again. I hadn't listened for a heartbeat.

"Are you alive again? Or are you a zombie?" I wanted her to be alive and well once again, but I knew the chances were slim.

"I'm not entirely sure, actually." Grams admitting that she

didn't know was disconcerting, to say the least. "I've never read about or heard of this happening before."

Bas stepped up behind me, bathing me in his heat. "I think you're technically a ghoul."

Grams narrowed her eyes at him. "You mean an evil creature that survives on the flesh of the dead? Are you telling me I will roam graveyards searching for food and become a rabid beast?"

I was shaking my head back and forth so fast I became dizzy and had to brace myself with a hand on Sebastian's chest. "She can't be a ghoul. I didn't cast a spell for one. I wanted to bind her soul to a body." Clearly, I hadn't thought that through. Of course, she would have gone back to her remains. That was her body.

"I don't think you created a ghoul. I don't feel anything malevolent coming off of her. And I don't feel her being animated by an outside source." Now that Violet mentioned it, I sensed only my Grams. Nothing more. That eased the vice around my heart. "We will need to research this more. But right now, we have bigger fish to fry." Violet was right. The rest of this could wait. We had to stop Vodor before he destroyed all of Pymm's Pondside and killed me in the process.

"Do we have time for me to change? I'm showing more flesh than a stripper." I wanted to laugh at the image Grams painted but couldn't. Scanning her more thoroughly, I saw that her dress decayed where her body hadn't. It looked like swiss cheese with all the holes in it.

"I can conjure you a tree of leaves," Theamise offered, startling me. "I'm glad you're back, Isidora. I've missed you."

I looked over to see her and Kairi watching the exchange. "I missed you as well and am pleased to see Fiona added a mermaid to Pymm's. I always wanted one to make their home in the pond. Ever since I was a little girl."

"Let's get you changed so we can kick Vodor out of our portal," I interrupted and headed for the back door. I had no idea how I managed to bring Grams back or if it would last. My gut was an uneasy knot. Instinct told me Grams and I had a lot of work ahead of us to undo what I'd done or keep her from becoming a flesh-hungry creature.

I shook my head at my life. Why had I ever thought bringing Grams back to help force Vodor back was a good idea or was going to be easy? Because I've lost my mind. I had to force the panic aside and roll with this magical twist. There was no other choice. I had more than my house on the line here.

## CHAPTER 5

I watched Grams climb the stairs far better than I remembered over the past five years. Her muscles and tendons should be nothing but mushy pulp beneath her skin, which shouldn't be intact at all. There was a reason I never considered her animating in her own body. It should be a goopy mess in the bottom of her coffin with little bits of hair clinging to her scalp.

I'd seen magic do some unbelievable things, but this topped them all. I had magically reconstituted Grams' body. Disbelief washed over me as I moved to follow her and tripped. The ground was coming up to meet me, and I was scrambling to catch my footing when strong arms banded around my chest.

I knew the feel of that hold anywhere. I glanced up and smiled at Sebastian. "Thank you so much. I'm afraid I would have landed on my face if you hadn't caught me."

Argies snorted from a few feet in front of me. "Of course, you would have. You just did something no one else can manage without killing themselves."

"What do you mean?"

Bas glared at the dragon shifter as I tucked my arm through Sebastian's elbow and started walking. "What Argies is trying to say is that there is a reason no one has ever heard of this happening. It takes more power than any being possesses. I'm not entirely certain of Vodor at this point, but I doubt it."

"Oh crap! What if he brings Thelvienne back to life? We tossed her rotting corpse through to him." My heart raced so fast in my chest I got dizzy."

Bas rubbed soothing circles on my back. "I don't know much about the process, but I don't think he can, even if he tried. There was nothing left in that body that resembled life. She decomposed like she did because she was rotten from the inside out. There is nothing left to bring back."

"Bas is right. If I had to guess, I'd say she turned to ash not long after you punted her back through the portal to Eidothea," Finarr added.

Violet shook her head. "One problem at a time, Fi. There is no reason to go borrowing trouble. We have more than enough in front of us."

"You're right. I need some coffee, so Grams and I can cast Vodor out. I'm running on a quarter tank." My entire body sagged and longed to crawl into bed. I could barely lift my hand to twist the back doorknob. How the hell was I going to perform a spell that would block Vodor from perverting the portal and using it to suck the power from me and my land?

Inside the backdoor, I made my way from the mudroom into the kitchen. My heart dropped when I didn't see my Grams. There was no noise coming from upstairs either. We'd been stupid to wait to get rid of Vodor.

I never should have allowed her to change her clothes. No one gave a crap if she wore a dress that had more holes than a honeycomb. Adrenalin dumped into my system, boosting my energy stores. "Grams! Where are you."

Sebastian ushered me further into the house. "She's upstairs. Can't you hear her making a..."

Bas was cut off by my grandmother shouting at me. "I'm in my bedroom." My heart dropped back inside my chest, where it continued pounding a million miles a second.

My legs carried me far faster than I thought they could as I hurried to the stairs and up them. I stopped short in my room when I saw her tossing clothes from the armoire onto the floor. She hadn't seen the closet I had magicked into existence with Camille's help.

"What are you doing?" I hadn't meant to use my 'mom' tone with her. It slipped out when I saw her making a mess of my stuff.

Grams rounded on me and thrust her hands on her hips. It hit me as she turned that she was slimmer in real life than as a ghost. And she had more wrinkles around her eyes and mouth.

It made me think that she chose how she appeared when her spirit returned. Or perhaps that was the age at which she started the spell I used to call her back from the other side. I'd have to ask her about that later. Right now, she was lecturing me.

"Are you even listening to me?"

Shaking my head, I entered the room and bent over to pick up the pile of sweatshirts. My bad knee protested, and I ended up sitting down on the edge of the bed. "I'm sorry I missed that."

"She's exhausted, Isidora. You know the spell she performed would have killed a normal witch or Fae." My head snapped up hearing Sebastian defend me to my grandmother. He was gruff and all hard edges. I never would have imagined him taking any steps to preserve someone else's feelings. Hell, he'd chastised me more than once about my ignorance and mistakes.

At first, I didn't like him because of it, but it made me grow thick skin right from the start and made it easier to deal with all the crap thrown at me. He forced me to look inside for the answers instead of asking or expecting someone else to come to my rescue.

Of course, he also came to my rescue when I was pulled to Eidothea and struggled to find my way back to Earth. I had the situation covered, but it still meant a lot to me that he returned to a place he had left behind to make sure I was alright.

Grams' shoulders stiffened as she continued to paw through my stuff. "I understand that, but how the hell am I supposed to function if I don't have anything to put on? I can't very well go around doing spells skyclad. I'm not sixty years old anymore."

I choked on the laugh that bubbled up my throat. "What was I supposed to do, Grams? Keep everything in your room as a shrine to you? You died and weren't supposed to come back to life. Are you even alive? Do you have a heartbeat? Most importantly, are you staying alive? There are so many unanswered questions, but the fact of the matter is I took over Pymm's Pondside because I knew it was what you wanted me to do."

"Now that I know there is no danger up here, I'm going to put on a pot of coffee," Bas announced once my little tirade ended.

"Do you even know how to make coffee?" I asked with a raised eyebrow. I'd never seen him cook anything. He was the master of a forge and poured a mean scotch. That was the extent of what I'd seen him do.

Sebastian graced me with a sexy smirk before he leaned down and placed a brief kiss on my lips as if we were officially a couple. I was wildly attracted to the guy, and that was as far as I'd gotten. Shit kept happening, and I hadn't had a chance to think things through.

*You aren't ready to admit you want more.* No, I wasn't. I'd had my one great love in life. You didn't get two, did you? "I think I can manage to put some grounds in the machine and fill it with water. It's not rocket science." Sebastian's reply distracted me before I could get lost down that particular rabbit hole. Once again, now wasn't the time to be thinking about a relationship. I had to save my home and family's legacy.

Violet chuckled at that. "I'll make something to eat. You need sustenance before you go back out there and do more magic."

Aislinn bobbed her head. "Yeah, we don't want you burning yourself out."

I focused on my grandmother while everyone else drifted out of the room. "Look, Grams. I'm sorry about all of this. It was difficult for me to pack your stuff up, but I had to move on. Keeping your clothing would have made it impossible for me to start to rebuild my own life here. I would have been crippled by grief every time I opened the cabinet."

Grams dropped the shirt she'd been holding on the bed and sighed. "I know you're right. I'm just not sure how to handle any of this. I knew you moved into my room before but seeing that I had nothing of my old life made me panic. I can only tell you my heart feels like it's all over the place, and so are my emotions. I don't know if I will live long, and I don't want to leave you again."

I stood up and wrapped my arms around my grandmother, noting how skinny she felt. It had been a long time since I felt the bones beneath her skin. "This is a new situation for everyone. I will move my stuff out after we are done casting Vodor out of our portal. And I will go to the shelter to see if they have any of your stuff left."

Grams shook her head, sending her long silver locks flying across my face before she pulled away from me. "No. This is your room now. I will use another and make do with what is here."

Giving her shoulders one more gentle squeeze, I let my arms drop. "We can figure this stuff out later. I have some leggings in the drawers, and there are other clothes in the closet here." I showed her the space Camille helped me create, then left her to get changed with an instruction to holler if she ran into any trouble.

Her breath had warmed my neck, and I felt her heart pounding in her chest. It was one reason I held on for so long. It reassured me to feel proof of life. Then the nurse in me couldn't ignore the erratic way it was beating. I wanted to grab my stethoscope and listen for more problems.

My phone rang, making me jump. I stopped before I shut the door and grabbed my cell from the top of the dresser. I was surprised to see Phoebe's name pop up on the screen. I hadn't talked to her in several weeks. She was the only one from my previous life I kept in contact with.

And for a good reason. Phoebe had been my closest friend in my previous life. I met her in college when we joined the nursing program and felt a connection with her immediately. Something between us clicked, and we became good friends right away.

She had been there for me when my parents died, when I got married, and when my kids had been born. We worked at the same hospital, but she was on the L&D ward. Her husband is one of the best heart surgeons in the country and sponsored me for ECMO training.

"Hey, Pheebs. How are you doing?" I didn't have time to chat with her. I needed to get this magical show on the road but didn't want to be rude to her, and I was the one that had answered the call without paying attention. I should have let it go to voice mail. It wasn't like I could hang up now.

"I'm sorry for calling so late, Fi." I heard a hitch in her voice and instantly felt guilty for not wanting to talk to her. "I have no one else to call and just needed to hear you tell me it is going to be alright."

I took a deep breath and entered the kitchen to find Violet stirring something in a ceramic bowl, Sebastian fiddling with the coffee pot, and Aislinn watching him while silently laughing.

"I am always here for you, hun. But I can't tell you it's alright when I don't know what happened. Back up and fill me in." I nudged Bas out of the way and winced when I saw the grounds underneath the filter.

"Miles wants a divorce. He's trying to take Nina from me when he's the one that was fucking that awful wench, Betina." Phoebe's voice hitched, and it sounded like she was choking. I guessed she was sobbing. I couldn't believe Miles slept with Betina. She was a general surgeon, and everyone knew she got around the hospital. My heart broke for Phoebe. I wished I was there to give him a piece of my mind.

"What an asshole," I told her.

"Right? I never imagined starting my life over at 43 and having to fight for my daughter. He told me I had to be out of the house by the end of the month, and I have no idea what I am going to do."

"You find a good divorce lawyer. Do you know where you're going to go?" Grams came downstairs in a black pair of my leggings and a sweatshirt that said, 'I have it all together; I just forgot where I put it.'

"I have a lawyer, but not sure how I am going to afford him and pay rent. I had to give him a ten-thousand-dollar retainer. That was everything I had in my savings account.

I'm sorry to unload this on you. I just don't have anyone here to talk to since you left."

I hated to do this to her, but I had to go. "I am always here for you, but right now, I have an emergency, and I have to go. I'm so sorry. I know you are going through a lot of crap right now."

Phoebe gasped, and I could imagine her waving her hands through the air in that animated way she had. "Don't apologize. It's my mess. Call me when you get the chance."

"You were there for me during the worst moments in my life, and I will be here for you. Speaking of which, you should take a vacation and come visit me." Grams stepped in front of me, waving her arms and shaking her head from side to side while mouthing, *she can't visit here*.

"I would love to, but I can't afford to be gone at the moment. As soon as I have time, I will hop on the first flight. I've always wanted to see the English countryside," Phoebe replied. "I will talk to you soon. Take care of yourself, Fi."

Guilt swamped me at the same time relief washed over me. "Don't forget what he did to you. He cheated and threw away the life you guys had built. Not you. Miles is good at making himself look like a king while keeping you beneath his boot." It was one of the things I hated about the guy. He wasn't good enough for Calista. She worked two jobs to put him through medical school, and he never treated her like the Queen she was. "Take care of yourself and call me anytime."

Violet was stirring the contents of the bowl so hard the batter went flying around the kitchen. "I can't believe that asshole did that to her." Violet and I had always been best friends, and she knew all about Phoebe and what I thought of Miles. "He should be castrated. Why can't men keep it in their pants? Does cheating on their wives and decimating the life they'd built really make them feel like better men?"

I shook my head. "He's an asshole, and I've always known it, but right now, we have another asshole to deal with."

Grams tugged at the bottom of the sweatshirt. I could tell she hated how tight the pants were and that her ass was so exposed. Thankfully, she didn't complain about it. "We need to do a reclamation spell and kick him out of our portal. And fast. I can feel the drain with each passing second. I think that's why my heart is so erratic."

If that was true, I might be able to keep her with me longer. I needed her by my side, teaching me all about my magic and how to wield it. "Then let's go do it."

Violet paused mid-pour and looked up with wide eyes. "Do you have enough energy? That last spell wiped you."

Sebastian came up behind me and started rubbing my shoulders. "I think you should give yourself a little break."

"We don't have time. What if the reason I am so exhausted isn't only because of the energy it took to bring Grams back? It might be because he's stealing what little I have. We do this now." I wasn't debating this with them and started for the door with Grams at my side.

The second we were outside, I saw that the destruction was so much worse behind the shimmer of my containment spell. "You ready?"

Grams bobbed her head and marched for the crypt, barely pausing to cross through the magical barrier. I glanced up at Sebastian. Without a word, he twined his fingers with mine, and we followed Grams.

I knew we were right not to wait when I passed through the shield with far less resistance than the last time. My spell was failing. Bas and I stopped next to my grandmother. She nodded at me. "On the count of three," I suggested.

"One," she murmured in reply, "two, three."

"*Repetere non habemus.*" The words left both of us at the same time.

To my surprise, a magical whip sliced through the air. It originated from my hand and hit foreign magic. The long, thin rope was purple and cut through Vodor's enchantment.

Instantly the suffocating feeling disappeared, and I was able to suck in a full breath. My skin wasn't pulled taught as if every drop of blood had been drained from my body. A second later, a concussive wave rolled through Pymm's Pondside, blowing my hair back and taking the dirty feeling with it.

"We did it." I was shocked at how easy that was with my grandmother by my side. I'd barely been able to touch his energy before.

"Don't sound so shocked, Fiona. You come from a powerful family." I laughed at Grams' chastisement. I'd missed that more than I would have thought.

"Looks like we have some rebuilding to do." The destruction stopped, and some of the tombstones returned to what they had been, but not all of them. Only the ones closest to the mausoleum showed signs of destruction. Even the plants were once again full of life.

The bones that formed the inner structure of the portal were reforming one piece at a time. The walls of the actual building had disappeared entirely, leaving only the foundation behind.

Grams waved a hand through the air, clearing the last of the stench. "We can tackle that together after we get something to eat. I'm starving. But before we go inside, let's do a protection spell."

I bobbed my head and let go of Sebastian's hand, and lifted both of mine into the air. The river in my core was close to overflowing now. "*Praesidio,*" I chanted without waiting for Grams. Purple lightning bolts left my palms and surrounded the bone structure. It looked like the walls were now made of pure energy before it sank into the scale.

I turned on my heel and wrapped an arm around my grandmother. The magic I used to bring her back had taken a lot out of me, but not as much as we thought. Now that Vodor was no longer draining me and the property, I could see that. The problem was I had no idea if that was a good or a bad thing.

# CHAPTER 6

Thoughts of being even more of a freak than my grandmother previously talked about vanished when I worried she would disappear on me. Okay, so that wasn't the most suitable description. I was downright terrified her soul was going to vacate her body, making it crumble to the ground in a massive puddle of goo and bones. At the same time, her ghost would float above while bitching about how she had died in my clothes.

None of us knew enough about the magic I used to bring her back to say what was going to happen, so I didn't bother voicing my concerns out loud. Instead, I held onto her hand tight and entered the house. The smell of freshly baked blueberry muffins filled the kitchen, making my stomach grumble.

"Gods, that smells divine! I never realized how much I appreciated how fresh pastries made the house fragrant." Grams let go of my hand and hurried to the island and snatched a muffin from the platter Violet had laid out. I joined her and inhaled deeply before selecting one of my own.

Grams finished her pastry in five bites, then shuffled to the stove, grabbed the teapot, and filled it with water. "It has been too long since I had a proper cuppa, as well. I was with your grandfather before you called me back, and we would have tea every morning while looking over the serene meadow outside our window. While it was beautiful and peaceful, I couldn't taste anything."

Aislinn placed the loose tealeaves on the counter and added the steeper. "What was heaven like? Was there a bright light and a tunnel?"

Grams made a pfft sound and shook her head from side to side. "There's nothing as absurd as a white light. I was aware I was dying when," Grams paused in explaining and brought a hand to her head. "I can't recall how I died."

I leaned one hip against the archway leading to the living room. "You mentioned you were killed when I first brought your spirit back. Do you remember who hurt you? You haven't said who it was."

She shook her head from side to side, and dirt flew from her hair. If she realized how filthy she was, she would be angry I let her go outside in such a state. Of course, everything changed when you came back from the dead. Perhaps, none of that mattered anymore. "My mind is blank when I try to bring up the memories."

"We need to find the *bilge* that is killing Fae in our town," Violet muttered. "I'd bet it was one of the king's assassins that got you, Isidora. Only a being of superior strength that is skilled at killing would be capable of getting the better of you."

"That's next on the list after taking Vodor off the throne." My to-do list was only getting longer the more time that passed. I might not be getting back to Phoebe anytime soon. Crap. I sucked as a friend. "Do you think we managed to hurt the king? I couldn't help but wish he was hit with a million papercuts on the guy while I was casting my spell."

Chuckles echoed around the room. "Papercuts?" Finarr asked with a furrowed brow. He and Argies were the only ones not laughing.

"They're tiny slices that barely open the skin, and they hurt like hell. It was the first thing that popped into my head while I was chanting to the spell to reclaim my land and my portal."

My grandmother let out a bark of laughter then. Her amusement was so infectious I found myself laughing right along with her. "If you had that in your mind while you directed your enchantment at him, he likely suffered the injuries. Serves the asshole right. You don't mess with a Shakleton woman."

"Can you imagine him sitting on his throne when his skin splits open all over his body, and his blood pours out? I hope his guards are searching for weeks to find the invisible culprit. But I think he uses illusion to intimidate and shake his opponents." I had to share the thoughts that had been racing through my mind.

Sebastian threw me a *what-the-hell-are-you-talking-about* look. "That magic couldn't have been an illusion, Butterfly. I felt the energy leave my body. It started to wither along with the plants. I know you experienced the same thing. You nearly collapsed."

"And you grounded me. I'm not saying the entire thing was his trickery. The depth of his destruction and ability to reach us is what I think was faked. Think about it. What had us panicking and reacting without a good sense of direction? It was the fact that it seemed like he was draining all of us and the land at a record pace."

Grams growled. My head snapped around. I'd never heard her make that kind of noise. "That's precisely what he did. I'd bet money he wanted you unhinged and scrambling so he could find a way to steal the portal out from under you. The fact that the bones reappeared without any intervention from us confirms your assessment. He found a way through, but he never had a foothold and certainly wasn't close to taking Pymm's Pondside from us."

Anger burned in my gut. I'd fallen right into his trap. Although I couldn't regret it entirely. It was fear over him taking my new life from me that forced me to bring Grams back from the dead.

"That's just like him," Finarr snarled. "He uses our weaknesses against us. He plays on a parent's fears for the children's safety, and they end up giving him their power without any effort on his part."

"So, what you're saying is that he's a lazy bastard on top of it all." It baffled me that this guy managed to take the throne when he didn't show any real power. And didn't care.

Sebastian laughed, surprising me. "He's always been a pompous blowhard. He was the last to master certain spells and didn't show much promise in school. But there was no one better at glamouring. It was one reason Thelvienne didn't give him the time of day back then."

Argies bobbed his head. "She only had eyes for you, Bas. It wasn't until you left the realm and Vodor took the throne that she noticed he even existed." Hearing about how the dead Queen was obsessed with Sebastian made me clench my hands into fists and bite my tongue, so I didn't make some snarky comment.

Was I jealous of the evil woman? *You're just now realizing that?* It wasn't surprising that my mind was behind my heart concerning Sebastian. I'd grieved Tim for six years now and hadn't allowed myself to consider anything or anyone else.

Many women felt like it would betray their spouse to move on, but that wasn't why I hadn't started dating again. I had no desire to play the games. Demurring and pretending to be someone else took too damn much effort for me. Having to always be on and putting my best foot forward. Besides the fact that you didn't really get to know each other for months until we both stopped putting our best foot forward.

"If you managed to embarrass him in such a way, he will really be out for blood now." I looked away from Sebastian's handsome face at the severe tone of Finarr's voice.

The blood froze in my veins. That didn't sound good. "I already knew he was after me. The attack proved that much."

Finarr bobbed his head. "Yes, but you didn't publicly embarrass him. You proved the Queen wasn't all that strong, to begin with. It upset him because he's always been obsessed with Thelvienne, and I think in his own twisted way, he loved her. But if you managed to injure him from another realm and anyone witnessed it, he will look like a weak King. The court will lose faith in him, and it will feed the rebellion, making them take action against him."

"There is no bigger sin in his eyes. Vodor is all about how he looks to others. It's why he's the best at casting illusions." Argies jumped in and added.

"How does that put me in even more danger?" I could see how that would piss a guy like him off, but I had upset him when I killed his wife, turning his attention directly on me. Before that, he had been aware of me, but I hadn't been his main focus.

"He will put every resource he has into hunting you down. He will find a way to send his troops through the portal to catch you in your bed and cut out your heart." Bas bared his teeth at Argies for being so frank with me.

I placed my hand on his arm and held it there until he turned to look at me. I held his gaze for a few seconds, falling into his dark eyes. "Okay, so we need to take action against him sooner rather than later. Is there anything you can suggest for me to protect myself against him? I'm not entirely sure if I did hurt him, but it would be good to know what I can do."

"I suspect that you have some resistance to his power which is why he tried another tactic and used the portal," Sebastian told me. "I've never seen him open himself to so much danger. I've seen Fae fall every day to his machinations. The fact that you haven't yet succumbed to whatever he has thrown at you creates enough of a risk. Your best bet is to mask your energy signature and scent."

"That's impossible to do," Grams argued. "A halfling can't hide their true identity, so even if she manages to cloak her signature, he will know it's her. No other hybrid would be stupid enough to enter Eidothea."

Argies sat on a stool and grabbed a muffin from the counter in front of him. "You're right, Isidora. He will know it's her immediately. We can't wait to take him out, or he will discover a way to get to you and take your power. If he obtains your power, there will be no way to stop him. It would be the worst outcome for all involved."

Butterflies swarmed in my gut, and my breathing turned shallow. I didn't want to go. I was just starting a new life and loving it, even with death and danger around every corner. I was excited about the idea of having my Grams there in person to teach me new skills.

"I'm going with you guys." My eyes flew open at my grandmother's statement. I just brought her back to life. I can't stand the thought of her being in danger.

"No, you can't leave Pymm's Pondside. Not only do we have little understanding of the enchantment that brought you back, but we don't know if and/or when it will fail. You need to stay here while the land is still vulnerable. Vodor might not have really been stealing our family's energy. Still, he found a new source of energy that weakens us in the process. He will keep trying to exploit that connection until I am too weak to fight him."

"Fair point. I'll stay, but what happens if the magic fueling my current existence is exhausted while you're gone? I will have no way to protect you or our home."

The thought of leaving Pymm's Pondside and all of Cottlehill Wilds vulnerable made me sick to my stomach. We already had one homicidal maniac on the loose. "We call in Camille, so she is here to back you, Aislinn, and Violet up should the worst happen."

Grams made a face. "I don't need that woman here. I will manage just fine without her, especially if I have these two with me."

There was something between the women that I didn't understand, and now was not the time to delve into the reasons. I had to reinforce Grams' life force before leaving and pray nothing happened.

"I'll cast protections over your body, focusing on your vital organs before we leave. But I need you to promise that if you start to feel off in any way at all, you will give her a call so she can come to protect the portal." It was all I could do at the moment.

Grams reluctantly nodded her head and set her empty teacup in the sink. "I won't let anything get in the way of protecting our home. Now, we have some spells to go over before you guys head out. I want to make sure you know as much as possible."

I nodded and dumped out the grounds Sebastian had put under the filter, then rinsed everything and put on a fresh pot of coffee. I needed the boost if I was going to get through this crap without falling asleep.

# CHAPTER 7

"You do realize we're going, right Fi?" I glared at Violet's announcement. The thought of her putting her life on the line made my stomach hurt worse. Maybe I was getting an ulcer. It wouldn't be a surprise. I'd been stressed out and hit with one emergency after another.

"You have to be here for Ben and Bailey. They need you." I hoped she listened to reason. I wouldn't be able to live with myself if anything happened to her.

"I'm not sure when you forgot that we're the Backside of Forty and in this together. We are both going with you." Aislinn stood there glaring at me with her arms folded over her chest.

I'd just gone around with my grandmother. I couldn't fight Violet and Aislinn, too. "Alright, but you listen to these guys if they tell you something. They're the experts on Eidothea, and we are all returning home on one piece."

Grams threw her hands up and made a scoffing sound. "So, you allow them to go, but not me. I'm a powerful hybrid on my own, Fiona. Perhaps I should remind you."

I rolled my eyes at her bravado. I knew it was difficult for her to be left out. She'd been out of the game for months and obviously wanted to be a part of it. Unfortunately, we couldn't afford my spell slipping and the portal being left vulnerable.

"You know why you can't come. Even if we could be assured the magic that brought you back wouldn't fail with you ending up dead again, I need you here to ensure Vodor cannot attack the portal again as a way to weaken me."

"I hadn't even considered that," Finarr blurted. "I've been so focused on getting back so we can wage war against him that I haven't processed the ramifications of him being able to drain you through the portal. We need to assume the fucker will hack into the magic and use it as a way to weaken you the second he knows you're in his territory."

Sebastian growled and started pacing. "Are there any additional protections you can cast to tighten the magic of the portal? We need all the layers we can add because Finarr is right. He got to you once using the veil against you and will do it again."

Shaking my head from side to side, I refilled my coffee cup. "I have no idea. I haven't exactly been studying."

"I'm not sure there is anything." I didn't like Grams saying that. She always had the answer. How could she come up empty at a time when I needed a Hail Mary? "There aren't additional enchantments in the family grimoire, but we should add additional layers of simple protection spells around both sides."

"I'm not sure I will have time to cast protections after we cross into Eidothea. Last time I was met with a troop of soldiers when I landed in the realm." One of Fodor's men had yanked me through the portal and lost his life in the process, but I was stuck there and had to take off running in a foreign place to avoid being captured or killed. My heart raced, and I got lightheaded just thinking about going back.

"Normally, you would have to be there to cast the protections on that side, but you forget you're a *nicotisa*. You can do it from here." Every time Grams reminded me I was this super powerful hybrid, I wanted to find a cave to hide out in. I had no idea what being a nicotisa meant other than it put a target on my back. The reality was I didn't have a clue what I was doing, and there were thousands, maybe even millions of Fae counting on me to save their realm. *No problem. Piece of cake.*

Setting my mug down, I bobbed my head and trudged to the door. "At least I'm getting all my steps in today."

Violet snorted as she smoothed her hair back from her face. "My legs are bitching at me that we don't need to get them in before eight am."

I couldn't help but laugh at Violet's joke. "Let's get this done, so we can pack and go save a realm."

For the umpteenth time since I was startled out of bed a few hours ago, I walked outside and crossed to the crypt. It was eerie to see the exposed bones. Next on the list after saving Eidothea was rebuilding this structure. The killer roaming Cottlehill Wilds would have to wait until that happened. We couldn't have the portal so exposed.

If I was lucky, Thelvienne was the killer haunting our streets. I refused to think about how unlucky I'd been lately and focused on calling up my river. It flowed readily through my veins.

I closed my eyes and tried to mentally trace the magic's path and get a picture of the weak spots. I was looking through a massive tunnel that made me think of the aorta and how it carried blood to the body.

Using that analogy, I recalled the countless AAA repairs I had assisted Miles with. Bringing up the metal-polyester graft image used to patch any tears or holes, I used the idea and applied it to the thin spots along the tunnel. I recall Violet and Aislinn both telling me that intent was vital to performing magic. It was the one factor that helped keep me focused. And I had to believe it worked. I might not be graceful and execute my spells flawlessly, but I managed to get close to the hoped-for results.

Grams grabbed my hand before I managed to cast. Looking down at her, I smiled. This was how I should have learned. With her by my side, assisting and directing me along the way. There were no guarantees she would be with me for long, so I appreciated her while I had her.

*"Praesidio et tranquillissimum,"* we both chanted at the same time. Energy flowed from our joined hands and traveled to the veil shielded by our ancestors. It vibrated, sounding like bees buzzing in a hive as it activated. The wind whipped around us, sending our hair flying into our faces before settling a few seconds later.

I brushed the red strands out of my eyes, surprised to feel my connection to the portal as a thick gold band where it was a thin ribbon before. It was like a second heartbeat, thrumming in my middle. I wasn't sure if that would leave me more vulnerable to an attack by Vodor or not. When I traced the tunnel's magic, I was surprised to find it covered in a thick layer of the patch.

"How'd you come up with the lining?" Grams asked as we released each other.

"You can feel that?" She hadn't told me to find the magic and follow it, so I wasn't sure if it was just me or not.

"I had no idea you'd done anything until you just pulled me into the energy of the portal. I've never experienced it from that perspective. It was almost as if we were standing inside the thing and evaluating it." I'd never seen the awed expression Grams wore at that moment.

"I didn't mean to pull you in with me. I thought about how doctors repair and reinforce weak walls of arteries, particularly the aorta, and applied that method to reinforcing the portal. That's why it felt like you were inside it because I traced the magic to get a picture of what we needed to do." I was babbling. I did that when I got nervous. Everyone was staring at me as if I'd grown another head.

"What?" I demanded.

Grams shook her head. "You have a unique way of looking at things. And this right here was proof of how powerful you are."

"Ordinary witches can't do that," Violet explained.

"The Fae can't either. At least not that I'm aware," Aislinn added.

"No. Fae can't get inside an enchantment and look around to evaluate it," Sebastian agreed.

I shrugged my shoulders then started walking back to the house. "Now that the holes are patched, we have some packing to do. I'm not going through without a bag this time. Can I bring one of your weapons, Bas? I'd feel better if I had something aside from magic to fight back with."

"Sure. I'll grab some supplies from my place and be back in a few."

Aislinn lifted a hand. "I could use a weapon, too, if you have one."

"I have a forty-five I'll bring." Violet owned a gun? How had I never known that about her? I didn't like them. I'd seen the damage they caused, most accidentally. Not to mention the fact that you are something like ten times more likely to be killed by your own gun.

"I'll grab you a dagger. Automatic weapons like that aren't reliable in the Fae realm." I gaped at Sebastian's announcement. I was learning new shit left and right today, and it wasn't even eight yet.

With weapons decided, we said our goodbyes and agreed to meet back at my house in an hour. I tried to settle my mind and focus on packing as I entered the house and climbed the stairs. I was going to the Fae realm to kill the king.

I'd never murdered anyone before killing Thelvienne, and here I was planning another death only hours later. The thought made me uneasy because I didn't regret what I'd done and wasn't hesitating to help ensure Vodor went down. They were evil to their core and exploited other creatures for their own selfish reasons.

* * *

A KNOCK on the door made me jump. My hand flew to my chest as I turned to see who was there. "Sebastian. I'm almost done here." I shoved another pair of socks and underwear in my backpack and considered the leggings and t-shirts I had laid out.

"I was hoping to talk before everyone else arrived."

Lifting my head, I nodded and set the clothes down. "What did you want to talk about."

"I know you don't want to hear this, but I'm worried about you going to Eidothea, where Vodor has all the power. You will be more vulnerable."

I cupped his cheeks, giving him a smile. "You can't wrap me in bubble wrap. I know it's difficult to see right now, but I do have some powers. I've done shit like bring Grams back, which frightens me, so I hold back at times. I have three kids to take care of and a new life to explore. I'm not about to hold back and let this asshole get the best of me."

Bas closed the distance between us and pressed his mouth to mine before he pulled away. I wanted to object and bring him right back. "I know you're a powerful, grown woman capable of making your own decisions, but I can't help wanting to keep you safe. It's not something I'm used to experiencing, and I'm not going to stop you. I just wanted you to know how I feel and why I will be stepping between you and danger. I don't want to go into battle without telling you that I'm all in. I want more with you. I know you have wanted time to get through these crises first, but I refused to go into this fight without letting you know how I feel."

It had been decades since I was overcome by those fluttery feelings. The way my heart opened wide hadn't happened since the early days with Tim and the births of my kids.

Without letting my mind talk me out of my reaction, I followed my gut and threw my arms around his neck, then jumped into his arms. He caught me and held my backside in his hands.

"I moved here to start my life over. It has been one major crisis after another, saving the adrenalin junky in me from getting bored and moving away. Still, it has made it difficult for me to think beyond today. I have to say that putting aside the fact that I got my magic and bringing my Grams back, you are the best surprise of all. You make me feel things I thought I never would again. And you brought me back from the dead. Literally. You set my body on fire in the best way possible."

A slow smile spread over his mouth. "In what ways?" He didn't wait for me to answer as his mouth took mine in a rugged, sensual kiss. His lips were harsh and bruising and made me wet faster than hot flashes made me sweat.

"Mmmm," I groaned against his mouth.

His hands tightened on my ass cheeks and tugged me taught against his body. I loved kissing him. It took me back decades and reminded me what new love was like. I understood why there were serial monogamists that went from relationship to relationship. I wanted to hold onto the passion flowing freely between us and hold it close.

Bas moved his mouth and nipped his way to my earlobe. "We'd better stop before this gets out of hand."

My brain was fogged with hormones and need. "Who says we have to stop? We have thirty minutes for a quickie."

His groan vibrated against my pounding pulse. "Don't tease, Butterfly."

Reaching between our bodies, I gripped his shirt in my fists and pulled up over his head. "I might not be ready to profess my undying love to you, but I know I want more, as well. And I don't want to go into this without feeling you inside me at least once. It'll give me something else to fight for."

I tossed his shirt aside, and my gaze became glued to the muscled planes of his chest. I'd never seen a more perfectly sculpted body in my life. My hands went to it like metal to a magnet.

"You are gorgeous."

Sebastian walked backward and laid me on my bed, then stood back and watched me closely. His hands went to my boots and pulled them off my feet before going for my pants and panties. I lifted my hips, giving him more access while also trying to raise my sweatshirt over my head.

Bas chuckled at my eagerness and shucked his shoes and pants next. I licked my lips. "Commando?"

Sebastian fell on me then and laid his body over mine. I still had on my bra and socks and probably looked ridiculous, but that didn't stop him from devouring my mouth. Something brushed over my clit a second later, and I gasped.

"Oh, God." I writhed and lifted and moved, trying to get more pressure where I needed it. At first, I thought he had run his finger through my slit until his cockhead nudged my opening.

"Need to make sure you're prepared for me," he murmured more as if he was reminding himself than talking to me.

I answered anyway. "I'm good to go. Never been more ready in my life."

He chuckled and retook my mouth, his tongue sliding against mine, mimicking how our bodies were joining. The pressure at my core increased then disappeared. I had no patience for this slow shit.

I lifted my hips at the same time he thrust back in, and I ended up impaling myself on his impressive cock. I sucked in a breath and stilled while my body adjusted. He was much bigger, and it had been a long time since I had been with a man. For a split second, my chest constricted. Tim was no longer the last guy I'd been with. The fact that I was with Sebastian and this wasn't some one-night stand got me right back on track.

Bas kissed down the side of my neck and went lower. Using his teeth, he tugged my bra cup lower until he exposed my nipple. His tongue was rather talented as he licked then sucked the hard bud into his mouth. Just like that, my arousal was through the roof.

My hips lifted to meet his as he set a fast and hard rhythm. I wasn't sure whether it was because it had been so long or because Sebastian's cock hit nerves inside me that had never been touched before. Still, I raced up the hill with my body coiling tightly.

My heart raced as I chased my climax. I couldn't think beyond the pleasure of the moment, which turned out to be a relief. I tended to get into my head, and I didn't want anything ruining this perfect moment.

Sebastian didn't try to make this an emotional encounter. Even his declaration to me wasn't all that touchy-feely. I'd bet anything he sensed too much would make me shut down at the moment and held back while still sharing what he needed to. I appreciated that he didn't push me or try to tell me what to do.

I arched my back, shoving more of my breast into his mouth while moaning loudly. I should worry Grams would hear and come to see what was up, but I was too lost in the moment.

My muscles clamped down on him when I felt one of his fingers reach between our bodies and press over my clit while he shifted his mouth to my other breast. It was enough to send me careening over the edge.

My orgasm exploded out of me, His mouth crashed down on mine, and he swallowed the way I screamed his name. He grunted and jerked above me seconds before I felt his seed shoot from him and into me.

I collapsed against the mattress and tried to catch my breath. "As much as I don't want to stop what we are doing, we should get cleaned up. The others will be here soon."

Bas withdrew, picked me up, and then carried me into my bathroom, where he flipped on the water. He finally removed my bra and took several steps away from me. "I'd better keep my distance, or we won't get through this shower."

I laughed and stepped beneath the spray. My body was languid despite the aches and pains. Now that the sex was done, my mind returned to what was ahead of us. The post-coital bliss evaporated and left me shivering as my heart started beating faster. We were walking into a war, and we might not all make it back.

# CHAPTER 8

I grabbed hold of my grandmother and held her tight. She patted my back and returned the embrace. She smelled like always, and her hug was close to the same. She was smaller, but I felt the love she had for me through our connection. It was enough to remind me I wasn't alone in the world, and no matter what, I still had her.

It would suck if I came back and she was back to being a ghost again, but I would rather have that than lose her forever.

"Don't worry about me. I'll be fine. And you will, too. You're a Shakleton, don't forget it. And don't let his pathetic illusions fool you. You can see through them."

I released her and brushed a tear away from my cheek. "He's nothing more than a power-hungry asshole. And there's a reason he has to steal magic and strength from others."

"Yeah, because he has none of his own," Aislinn added with a snort.

Violet adjusted the straps on her backpack and tugged on

the straps over her shoulders. “He probably has a small dick, too. He has to be compensating for more than being weak.”

“He’s small in every sense of the word.”

“Grams!” I couldn’t believe she was joining in the ribbing. She’d always told Violet and me it was crass to talk about sex and sexual organs like we did. “How would you know he’s small?” I couldn’t help but wonder at the certainty in her tone.

“I wasn’t always married to your grandfather. And I was gorgeous in my youth.” Grams crossed her arms over her chest and cocked one hip to the side as she struck an indignant pose.

“You still are. Please tell me you didn’t sleep with him.” My stomach rebelled at the thought.

Grams’ expression screwed up into a grimace as she shuddered. “Hell no. I wouldn’t touch him with Camille’s hands. Vodor tried to seduce me and was brazen in his attempts to get me into his bed. I have never been stupid or naïve. Now, remember your offensive spells and attack before your enemy has a chance to hit you with a stun spell.”

Emotion clogged my throat, making it impossible to respond right away. I loved her so much, and there was a good chance she would die before we returned. This might be the last time I was able to hug her. It was surprising how difficult it was to walk away when you were looking at the end.

I’d wasted so much time before she passed away. I should have visited more often. *Hindsight is always 20-20. There is no changing the past, only taking what you learn and making different choices in the future.*

“I won’t forget. Are you guys ready?” Each of my friends nodded, and I centered my mind, pushing aside the need to hold onto Grams and never let go.

I climbed the two steps and glanced up as I passed

beneath the archway of skulls. There was no door to open and no walls hiding what I was doing. It felt weird to be out in the open while dealing with the portal. It had been protected from view for centuries before Vodor destroyed the building around it like a two-year-old throwing a tantrum. Thankfully, even if anyone was watching from the shadows, they wouldn't be able to make it work. No one outside the family would be able to open the passage.

I walked into the open space and noticed the stone sarcophagus was still there. We'd have to recreate the stained-glass window that decorated the upper section of the far wall.

Lifting my hands, I chanted the spell to open the portal. Faster than ever before, an oval appeared and hovered in the middle of the room with light surrounding it. When I looked at the image, it was disorienting to see the woods around Pymm's Pondside with the Fae world overlapping it.

It made my eyes cross and reminded me of those images made up almost entirely of one number or letter. You had to pick out the different one. I turned when I heard footsteps. The others joined me in the open structure, and together, we scanned the view on the other side.

The bright green, almost neon grass was serene, and the trees were placid. I didn't even see a brownie. Like usual, the sweet scent of flowers carried on the breeze through the opening.

"Do you think there is an army waiting to ambush us?" My hand tightened around one of the knives Bas had made me. It reminded me of an *Ogun* blade. It looked like an elongated arrowhead with a handle that had intricate braiding on it. My son collected different knives, and this style was one of his favorites.

Finarr rolled his head, cracking his neck. "I think we have to assume they're there and hidden behind a glamour."

Aislinn held her dagger with both hands and shuffled her feet. Violet held her blade loosely at her side while staring at the Fae realm with steely eyes. "We're ready." I'd known Violet my entire life.

"As much as I want you guys to stay here and stay safe, I'm glad you're here with me," I admitted.

Violet smiled then. "Womb to tomb, baby. The Backside of Forty will always have your back." I laughed at our motto, 'womb to tomb.' When my parents moved me away, Violet and I swore a pact with each other that we'd always be friends, no matter what. And we had. For many years it meant expensive long-distance phone bills and summers spent with Grams. Social media made staying in touch simple.

"Agreed. Although, I hope things get a lot less dangerous soon." Aislinn's words were clipped, and her chest was rising and falling rapidly. I hoped she didn't hyperventilate.

"See you on the flip side," Argies called out before he and Finarr stepped up to the passage then walked through. I didn't see them in Eidothea, and it made me wonder how long it would take for them to travel there. Given the way Kairi and Finarr had stepped right through when they came to Earth, I expected it to be instantaneous.

The seconds passed incredibly slowly, making me grind my teeth. When they appeared with their weapons raised, I breathed a sigh of relief. It was clear they were trained for battle as they immediately scanned the area, then turned to face us and nodded.

"You two go next. Fiona and I will be right behind you."

"Put your weapons away. The first time I went through, I fell. The last thing we need is for you guys to stab yourselves by accident."

Violet gave me a 'duh' look. "You were pulled through by one of the King's soldiers, but I'd rather not take the chance."

Both of them tucked their weapons in the big pocket of their packs, then clasped hands and walked through the passage.

I turned to Grams and pulled her into another hug. "I love you so much, Grams. I can't wait to get back and learn potions and spells from you."

"Love you to the moon and back. I'll be waiting for you to return..." Shouting cut Grams off.

"Time to go, Butterfly." Sebastian's voice was deep with a growl to it. I gasped when I saw the soldiers fighting my friends.

"Be careful, Fiona." Grams' voice was cut off when I sucked in a breath, and we entered the portal.

Between steps, darkness encompassed me, and my hair whipping around my head in the wind created in the portal. I was surprised to find it easier to breathe this time. It had to be the opposing forces that cut off my ability to get oxygen to my brain and body the first time I went through the thing.

Adrenalin dumped into my system as I went through the dark tunnel. My mind conjured a million horrible sights I would see when we landed in Eidothea. My friends were fighting Vodor's soldiers, and I couldn't stop thinking they would be killed.

Before I got so carried away that I was hyperventilating, lights flashed around me, making black spots dance in my vision. The next thing I knew, I was being squeezed through a tight space. The compression around me disappeared, and I braced myself for what came next.

The sound of fighting and shouting reached my ears at the same time I was unceremoniously dropped onto a sunny, grassy field—*nothing like failing on your bad knee when your friends were literally fighting for their lives.* Thank God I hadn't fallen on the knife I still clutched in my hand.

Sebastian sprung to his feet immediately, pulling me with

him. I tightened my grip on my weapon and followed behind him as he rushed to help our friends. There were at least a dozen soldiers.

One of them stepped away from the group, drawing my attention. I diverted to tackle him. Either he was chickening out and trying to get away with his life, or he was up to something. A fist came flying toward me, and I had to dive forward. I'd seen actors lunging into smooth summersaults on movies and tried to execute the same move.

"Gah!" I screeched when my head hit hard and was forced to the side. I tumbled more than rolled and swung my knife as I cleared the ground. I managed to nick the Fae chasing me and avoided getting hit in the face. Unfortunately, he managed to stomp on my thigh. A loud crack echoed right before pain stole my breath.

"Ah, it's the half-breed Mundie," the Fae that had stepped away observed.

I pushed to my feet with great effort and tossed a fireball at him while I was standing up. It hit him on the side of his left leg. Payback's a bitch. It gave me time to punch the soldier coming after me. I braced myself and cast a shield around my body. I wasn't expecting it when his fist flew into my face. Forking hell, that hurt.

Pain exploded, and my vision was cut off in my right eye. I dropped my weapon as I fell to the ground and waited for blood to pour from the injury. Nothing happened, and I tried to crawl toward my friends. I didn't make it far when the first soldier limped toward me and grabbed a fistful of my hair.

I bite back the scream that wanted to escape. I had no desire to distract Sebastian when he was in the middle of three guards. I needed to develop a plan about striking out at more than one of them while healing my leg and eye. The heaviness and pain in the right side of my face told me I likely had a hyphema. If I didn't lower the pressure, I could lose my vision.

Grams' advice popped into my head, and I tossed out a stun spell. It was the first thing that came to mind. My jaw dropped when the soldier in front of me laughed and lifted an amulet. My chant was sucked inside and didn't do a thing to the guy.

My heart kicked into overdrive. I cast a healing spell and felt it tingle through my face and leg. These bastards were relentless, and my progress was cut short when one of them grabbed a fistful of my hair. Instinctually my hand flew to the top of my head. Needing to get free before I was killed, I clawed at his hands and fought to get free. That didn't bode well for us. He yanked hard, and I swear he tore out a chunk of my hair. Asshole! My thick locks had thinned out quite a bit with age. The last thing I needed was to lose anymore.

I needed to catch them off guard. My fire burned the first guy leaving behind the smell of his singed flesh. Scrabbling with one hand and trying to keep them from pulling me away from my friends, I lowered the other and touched his leg while releasing my fire. I was immune to my flames and didn't need to worry I would catch fire when I lit the asshole holding me on fire.

He shouted and let me go while bating at his hand and leg. The other soldier jumped in and wrapped beefy arms around me. I twisted and turned and tried to reach the second blade in my backpack but didn't get very far.

Violet's scream pierced the afternoon and froze my blood. It was a blood-curdling sound filled with pain. Looking over, I saw her holding one shoulder while blood poured from a large gash over the top. I saw white poke out from the middle of the gore.

Rage filled me. I refused to let these jerks take my best friend from me. I inhaled and held my breath along with the energy building in my chest. I released it in a loud scream and grimaced when the soldier holding me exploded in a shower of blood, bones, and guts.

Rather than waste any time, I raced for my friend and snatched my knife from the grass as I went. My arm was in motion when I reached Violet's side. The blade sliced through a guard's neck, making him release Violet to grab his wound.

I kicked him in the chest and sent him into another soldier while closing the distance to Violet at the same time. From the corner of my eye, the guard I burned was running for us, and two others had diverted from attacking Finarr and Argies. It was then that I saw Aislinn was sandwiched between the two Fae.

That eased the knot in my gut. I was building up to an explosion if I didn't find her soon. "Are you okay?" I assessed the injury and made note the white was bone. It was deep and made me wonder if she would be able to keep the limb. I couldn't treat her here, and I didn't think there were any hospitals.

Violet was a concerning shade of grey, which told me more than her words. "I'll be alri...watch out!"

My hand shot out to my side automatically, and the bomb left my hand before I had fully formed the thought. When there wasn't an explosion, I realized the soldier must have used an amulet.

It had distracted him enough that I was able to plunge the knife into his chest then yank it out. Violet no longer held a weapon. I didn't recall her having one in her hand, so maybe she hadn't been able to retrieve it from her bag. She'd been vulnerable because I didn't want them crossing with knives in their hands.

I stabbed out at the soldier, darting forward but never really making a move. "They can get through my shields, and they aren't using many spells. Can you access your magic? I don't think they will be able to absorb your power."

"I can't feel anything but the pain."

Keeping my knife in motion, I directed my thoughts toward Violet and her arm, knitting back together. "*Sana*." I shoved the spell toward Violet as I cast it.

"Shift into your dragon and fry these fuckers," Aislinn called out.

That got everyone's attention, and I could cast a bomb between the two facing Violet and me. I turned and covered her with my body a split second before they burst into a shower of Fae goo.

"Holy crap, that was awesome."

I lifted off of my bestie, happy the strain was eased from her voice. "How's your arm?" I watched as Sebastian, Finarr, and Argies were able to corral the remaining four soldiers and take care of them.

"It's not completely healed, but now I'll be able to keep it. It was hanging by a thread before."

Aislinn ran to us and lifted her arms to hug Violet, then let them drop. Approaching her side, I decided to focus on helping her rather than the screams and squelching sounds of blades cutting through flesh.

The wound was still dangerously deep, so I took out one of the t-shirts I'd packed and used my knife to cut it into strips. "This is going to hurt, but I need to bind it together and cover it so it protects against bacteria." After tying them together, I wound the fabric under her arm, over the wound, and around the opposite shoulder.

"Did you see them absorb the spells?" Aislinn asked a second before the guys joined us. "Was that why they weren't casting magic of their own?"

Sebastian brushed the hair that had fallen from my ponytail out of my face. "They actually were using enchantments, just not as often as they were their weapons. I'd bet Vodor sucked their energy when he crossed the portal and left them depleted."

"I really hate that guy. He's such an asshole," Aislinn muttered.

I bobbed my head in agreement. "Me too. Let's get out of here before anyone else shows up. I think one of them tried to send a message asking for reinforcements."

My body hurt, but this time I managed to escape with minimal injuries while my best friend had nearly lost her arm. I wanted to send her back home while we were close to the portal but knew better. She wouldn't want to leave Aislinn and me. I needed to do a better damn job of protecting them both.

# CHAPTER 9

"I'm not leaving the portal here." Vodor and his soldiers knew where it was located, and if I could manage to move it, I would eliminate the king's threat of using it against me. The last thing we needed was for him to sap my energy in the middle of a fight.

Sebastian shook his head as we stood at the edge of the tree line. "You're injured and need to focus your energy on healing yourself. Once Vodor is off the throne, there will be no reason to worry anyway."

I thrust my hands on my hips and glared at his too handsome face. "You're not as smart as I thought if you believe that will be the end of all the strife. Those who believe in him and are true followers will retaliate and plan another coup after we succeed. Besides, if I move it, I remove Vodor's ability to hurt me through it."

Bas sighed, and his expression softened. "You have a point there. What can I do to help?"

"Keep watch while I find the object that anchors the portal in this location and tether it to me."

Aislinn pointed to a spot beneath a cluster of dead Fae in

the clearing. "I noticed the top of a curved stone while we were fighting for our lives and wondered what it was and why it was buried where we crossed. Could that be it?"

Hope surged in the face of what had seemed like an impossible task. There wasn't much in the area, and I wasn't even sure where to start. It never occurred to me to look below ground.

I hobbled forward, and after two steps, strong arms banded around me and lifted me. "At least let me carry you. Your leg is hurt."

I rolled my eyes. He'd warned me he would want to protect me. Now wasn't the time for that. Besides, I preferred not to get distracted by the deepening relationship between us. Once I went down that rabbit hole, I wouldn't emerge until I sorted all my mixed emotions. "So is yours. Put me down. I can walk on my own."

Bas grumbled under his breath but set me down. Fortunately, we had made it to the spot Aislinn had pointed out. I opened my senses and was immediately hit with the signature of the portal, as well as death. The stone might be associated with the portal, but I couldn't get an accurate take on it.

"I need to clear out these bodies to get a better read." Sebastian bent to pick one up right when I tossed fireballs at them.

Jumping back, he glared at me. "You could have warned a guy."

Cradling his face, I pressed my lips to his. When I went to pull away, he stopped me and deepened the kiss. The heat from the growing flames added to the passionate moment. I tried to remember why this was a bad idea. Instead, I threw myself into the kiss and wrapped both arms around him.

"Now is not the time to start making out," Violet admonished. "And I wouldn't recommend getting down and dirty in the middle of a field where we just killed a dozen soldiers."

My cheeks heated as I broke away from Sebastian. When I turned to Violet, I noticed the bodies had been moved ten feet away and were now burning in a massive bonfire. "Thanks for taking care of that."

With the area was cleared, I was able to connect to the portal. The signature floated in the air a couple feet behind us. Still, the majority of the energy was beneath the ground. "Good catch, Aislinn. This is definitely what has tied the spell to the spot."

A groan left me when I bent to uncover the rock. Sebastian was there immediately and helping me to my knees. I let that one go and started digging. Gras and dirt flew to the side. I still hadn't uncovered the entire piece a few seconds later. How big was this thing?

Aislinn joined me while Violet stood aside and watched. I was glad she didn't try to help with her arm still in pretty bad shape. Every second we spent out in the open, my heart rate increased. It was only a matter of time until more soldiers arrived.

I needed to figure out if this was going to be possible. I couldn't carry a massive boulder with us. Accessing my magic, I called up my connection to the earth element then realized I had no idea what I was doing.

I looked up at Sebastian, who was standing sentinel above us. "I'm trying to use my earth element to see how big this thing is, but I have no idea what I'm doing. Can you help?"

He pursed his lips then knelt next to me. "Direct that energy toward the object you know holds the portal magic. Trace it with that elemental power. You should get a picture in your mind."

I liked that he didn't simply take over and do it for me. He had been paying attention and knew that I preferred to know how to do things. Closing my eyes, I did as he instructed and was shocked to find a horseshoe-shaped arch. And it seemed massive.

"It's a big arch made of stone, so it's hollow in the middle."

Aislinn stopped digging and brushed her hands together. "Let's use magic to move the soil. I don't want to linger here any longer. With the five of us, we should make short work of this."

Sebastian stood and offered me his hand. "Is that a good idea? Carrying a large stone archway will be a pain in the ass."

"We're doing it." Looked like the honeymoon was already over. And we hadn't really even begun.

To my surprise, Bas bobbed his head and gave me a peck on the lips. I stood stunned for a second before I lifted my hands and accessed my elemental power. Flames immediately flared to life in my palms. It wasn't a surprise because I had an affinity for fire.

Aislinn had explained that all Fae could connect with and use each of the elements. However, most had an affinity for one element in particular. It took effort for me to connect with the earth element.

Once I did, I used it to direct the dirt and grass to shift up and away from the stone. My pile grew while the others joined me. I freaking *loved* magic. What would have taken a backhoe a couple of hours was done in less than ten seconds.

We stood at the edge of the crater we'd created and looked at the object in the middle. The arch was at least twenty feet tall and had been engraved with runes along both sides. Before Sebastian could talk me out of it, I lifted the arbor and settled it over us.

"Let's replace the dirt and get the hell out of here." Aislinn, Finarr, and Argies immediately got to work while Sebastian stared at me for a second before complying.

Instead of helping them, I tethered the archway to me and tried to heft it into the air. It took several tries to get air to do what I wanted.

After a few seconds, I was pretty confident using the air to make it float and push it along with us. Violet reached out and touched the side closest to her. "This is unlike anything I've ever experienced. I've seen more magic since you came home and unbound your powers than throughout my entire life."

Sebastian rubbed his hands together then placed one on my lower back. "I can carry you that way you can heal and concentrate on keeping the portal with us."

I shook my head from side to side. "Nope. I've got this."

Bas fell into step beside me as I crossed to the forest. The second we reached the trees, I realized I'd need to turn it sideways so it was slim and wouldn't pose a problem maneuvering through the area. With a flick of my finger, I directed air currents to the front of the arch and sent it sideways so we didn't have to pause.

We walked in silence for half an hour. We were all tired, and I was adjusting where I sent my energy to keep the arch floating alongside us. Our progress was slowed because of it, but in the end, it would be best to have it moved to a new location.

Violet cradled her arm as we traipsed through the forest. "This reminds me of the time we went camping on Pymm's Pondside when we were fourteen years old."

"If you don't include the battle, injuries, death, and blood. But we were lost then too." At least the weather wasn't cook-an-egg hot. The walk was wearing on everyone. None of us had gotten away from the fight unscathed.

My leg was killing me, making me wonder if it was broken after all. Sebastian had been right about the drain pulling the portal along with me was taking on my body.

Oddly enough, my power level never reached critical levels. There was plenty of magic flowing through my veins.

Bas brushed a bug off his leg. It had landed close to a cut that hadn't stopped bleeding. "You two were never in danger. I'd have led you back before anything happened. Let me carry you. You'll heal faster."

I hadn't had time to really process the fact that we'd had sex right before crossing to Eidothea. Still, Sebastian had no problems knowing where he stood regarding me. He hovered and tried to do everything for me—something he never would have done before.

"No. We need to remain alert. More soldiers could find us any second. But more importantly, you watched us while we were out here?" Violet and I had been particularly boy crazy at fourteen, and I had no doubt we talked about something idiotic and embarrassing.

"I should have known you'd be out there," Violet interjected before Bas could reply. "I used to have the biggest crush on you, so it's probably good I didn't consider it. I might have tried to talk Fiona into hunting you down."

Sebastian lifted a low-hanging branch out of my way while watching me closely. "I've never been more grateful that Isidora put that spell on you," he told Violet. "Otherwise, I'd have been forced to listen to more inane chatter."

My jaw dropped to my chest, and I rounded on Bas. "What did you just say? What spell did my grandmother put on Violet? And why?" It wasn't a topic we'd discussed yet. I wondered why she'd been able to keep her true identity from me for so long. It made no sense.

Sebastian winced and cast me a sheepish look. It didn't belong on his face. He was always so self-assured and confident. "I should have thought that through better. All I can tell you is what I overheard and observed. I knew she bound your powers, and until recently, I assumed it was because your parents were taking you to live in an all-human city. Three-year-olds are all impulse and no control. That's one reason few of our kind live close to humans."

I sighed, then screeched when the arch slammed into the branches of a tree. My hands flew up as if I could catch the heavy hunk of rock. Sebastian and Argies caught it before it snapped the thing in half. It was then that my brain finally rebooted, and I called up my air element and steadied the passage.

I wiped the sweat from my forehead. "I've got it. Sorry about that. I actually forgot I was hauling this thing along with us." Despite the strain hoisting, this was on me long-term. I had been so distracted by hearing how far my grandmother went to hide the magical world from me.

That confused me more than anything. Here she was now encouraging and teaching me how to gain control and grow stronger. Logically, I knew she had protected me when I was younger, but I saw how much I had missed out on by not knowing about this world. If she had taught me from the beginning, I wouldn't be so vulnerable now.

"Back to the topic. You watched Violet and I make a tree fort?"

Bas chuckled. "From the way I remember it, you guys didn't erect a tree fort so much as spread some blankets on the ground."

I smacked his shoulder while Violet and I laughed with him. "Hey! We tried. We were only fourteen, and neither of us knew anything about construction."

"Really? I never would have known you weren't general contractors." Sebastian snorted. Actually, freaking snorted. I sounded like a pig when I did it, yet it was sexier than ever coming out of his mouth. "You carried one-two by four between you and had no tools. I think the board is still leaning against the oak."

Violet fluffed her hair, then groaned and dropped her arm. She hadn't been using her injured arm, but the movement must have caused pain in her other shoulder. "Our skills lie elsewhere. And if you saw so much of our night, I'd say you appreciated those skills, even back then. Otherwise, you wouldn't have been stalking us."

Sebastian's cheeks turned pink, and the sight made me smile. Alright, so it wasn't precisely pink. It was more of a flash that was there and gone before anyone could notice. It was a small glimpse at his softer side.

"As if I'd let a couple young giggling girls, Isidora and Lauren's girls at that, run into trouble. When your Grams gave me the land, I agreed to help her protect Pymm's Pondside."

Aislinn kicked a rock and sent it flying ahead of us. From somewhere in the bushes, we heard a high-pitched shout. "Oops. Sorry about that," she called out to whatever had objected. No one seemed to react or get worried, so I let it go. "I missed out on so much being so far behind you guys in school."

I glanced sideways at Aislinn. She was thirty-nine to my forty-two, almost forty-three. "Can you imagine the trouble we would have gotten into?"

"Trouble with a capital T. And chocolate," Violet said. She was smiling, but there wasn't much amusement in her voice.

"Speaking of, we need to do another Girl's Night where we do dessert for dinner. I love those nights." Aislinn's face took on a faraway look, and a smile spread across her face.

I laughed at that. "You know you're an adult, so we can have dessert anytime we want."

Aislinn waved her hand through the air and jumped quickly over a fallen log. I envied how smoothly she moved. Those three years made a *huge* difference. "I know we're adults, but the calories consumed during Girl's Night don't count. Everyone knows that. If I stuff my face with an entire chocolate cake all alone, I'm wracked with guilt, and my pants are instantly tighter."

"I'm pretty sure you don't gain weight that fast, but I finally know what you mean. Before moving here, Phoebe and I were too busy to go out much, and when we did, it was all about drinking wine and not about deserts. Before you two corrupted me, I couldn't imagine a night with no wine or tequila would be fun." I paused at the log and sent it over before I lifted one leg over. My feet slipped before I managed to get the other across, and I ended up jump hopping, so I didn't impale myself on the short branch beneath me.

Sebastian flew over and grabbed my arms to pull me the rest of the way. Argies helped Violet, and before long, we were on our way again.

"How much further?" Violet asked, reminding me of my kids on long car rides.

"We have a way to go, but we can take a break," Argies responds. "We could all use some food, too. I'll go find some fruit while you guys settle down."

I used air to maneuver the heavy portal and prop it against two massive evergreen-looking trees and sank to my butt. Bas settled next to me and started rubbing my leg in silence while I got out the bag of muffins I'd brought. No way was I eating what passed for fruit in Eidothea.

## CHAPTER 10

"Are we there yet?" Aislinn tossed the stick she'd been swinging into the bushes off to the side. My mouth flew open to warn her the second her arm had cocked back, but she didn't put much effort into the throw. Seemed like she remembered the rock hitting some poor creature before, after all.

"Five minutes closer than the last time you asked." I used to think maybe Argies was into Aislinn, but now I had to wonder. His reply didn't have any of the previous heat that had flared between them.

Aislinn bared her teeth at him. "Thanks, Captain Obvious. I was looking for a real estimate. I've never received one, and I need something to motivate me beyond protein bars and what passes for fruit here."

Argies sighed and wiped the back of his hand over his forehead, smearing dirt that was there in the process. "It's impossible to give you an accurate estimate, Princess. What with having to alter courses every hour or so. It seems like Vodor has all of his men roaming the forests, making it nearly impossible to avoid being caught."

"Too bad we aren't close to Midshield. Now is probably the perfect time to lay siege to the castle and kill Vodor. He can't have many surrounding him with how often we are running into his fucking soldiers." Finarr wasn't wrong about that, but we were in no shape to attack at the moment.

We were all a sweaty freaking mess, tired and hungry. My heart went from trotting to galloping as I waited to see if Sebastian and Argies would push to divert our course. The archway slipped, and branches snapped above, drawing everyone's attention. "That was me. Sorry. I lost my hold for a second. I'm good now."

"Let's take a break. I could use a breather." We'd been walking most of the day, and Violet needed to stop more often than the rest of us. She was breathing hard as she spoke, and her coloring hadn't improved much.

"Sounds good to me." We stopped where we were because we hadn't been traveling on any kind of road. I was utterly lost and relying on the guys to get us to our destination safely. It wasn't something that came to me naturally. As much as I tried not to, I usually stepped up and took the lead in situations.

"Let me check your shoulder." I settled the archway against the trees and turned to Violet.

She was hot to the touch and shivering. I wanted to curse our predicament. She likely had an infection and would become septic because we were in an alien world, and I couldn't access antibiotics.

"That thing has a heartbeat of its own now," Violet grumbled. "And it hurts worse now than it did before."

Unwrapping the makeshift bandage, I held back my curse when I saw the puffy, red skin around the edges of the wound. I tugged her top aside and noticed the red streaking from her injury and down to her chest.

I looked at Sebastian and shook my head slightly. "I need

some water. Can you get my water bladder out of my backpack?"

He peered over my shoulder and his lips pursed. "No problem. Finarr, can you find me some calendula and goldenrod?" He handed me the pouch. I pressed the mouthpiece and squeezed the bag so the liquid dribbled over Violet's wound.

Violet sucked in a breath, pressed her head into the tree she was leaning against and closed her eyes. "It's infected, isn't it? That's why I can't stop shivering."

I jumped as if she'd burned me with her question. "I think it might be, but we are going to take care of it. Or I can send you home right now. I can open the portal and get you home right away."

I wanted nothing more than to open it and send her packing, but I couldn't. It had to be her choice. I wouldn't take that from her unless her life was in peril. Then I would make a choice for her.

Pressing my fingers to her wrist, I took her pulse and placed my ear to her chest to listen to her heart. To my relief, a strong, steady beat echoed throughout her chest. Her magic reached out and tingled beneath my cheek. She had always felt like a cool breeze to me.

At least, that's how my mind interpreted her energy. Even before I knew she was a witch and had magic. Aislinn felt like water to me. Like the waves crashing against the cliffs close to her house.

Now, though, Violet felt more like a raging tempest. No longer a cool breeze, she was hot and blasted against me, leaving behind a slight sting. I wondered if that was the infection manifested. It didn't seem like the reason, but I couldn't really be sure. I just knew Violet wasn't the same, and I hoped whatever Bas had planned would stop any infection from getting worse.

"What are you doing with those plants? Making a poultice?" I vaguely recalled reading about herbs and their uses in my family's grimoire but hadn't memorized all of the details. I remembered that goldenrod was used in a gout remedy and to help with hemorrhoids of all things. I'd bet it had an anti-inflammatory property.

"Yeah. I'm going to make something we can put on to kill any infection that might be there," Sebastian explained.

Argies was standing as far from Aislinn as he could get, yet still staring at her. "We don't have medicine like you think of it here. It's all plant and magic-based. I know many healers but never picked up the craft myself. I assume you know one to cast of the salve."

Sebastian shrugged his shoulders. "I'm not actually going to do anything. Fiona is going to enchant it."

It was a sad state of affairs that my only reaction to this was to bob my head and start running through the best spell to use. "I've never done it before, but it can't be any harder than killing the Queen."

Violet laughed. The sound anemic. "If anyone can do it, you can. You're Grams is right, you know. You're the most powerful person I've ever met."

Emotion closed off my throat, and I had to blink away the tears that formed in my eyes. It meant everything to hear Violet's faith in me. "You can't know that for sure. We shouldn't place too much weight on what she's said." I didn't want all of Eidothea placing their expectations on me. It was too damn much pressure. It was better to have more to share the burden with. I could barely handle the portal. I didn't need anything else.

"It's true, though. I've been given a portion of your power, and it changed me." Violet and Aislinn mentioned feeling different than before. I hadn't stopped to think about all the ramifications of what that meant. "At least it feels like it did anyway."

Sebastian put his big, strong hands on my shoulders and rubbed the tension that knotted the muscles. "We all have a part to play in freeing the realm. You aren't in this alone, Butterfly, but don't underestimate yourself. Ah, thank the Gods you're back," Bas said to Finarr before I saw him through the trees.

"It wasn't easy to find them both. I found some bark we can use to grind them together, as well." Finarr held up the u-shaped piece of wood.

"Thanks. I had planned on crushing them in my hand, but this'll be easier." Sebastian took the plants and knelt. Finarr lowered himself beside Bas, and the two used rocks like a pestle and crushed the flowers.

Bas looked up at me and smiled. "Can you add some water? Not too much," he added when I bent down and squirted some on their mixture. It was a paste that was on the drier side until I added some liquid. "That's good," Sebastian said, stopping me from adding any more. The end result was a thick goop.

Aislinn was leaning over me when I stood up. "You just smear that on the wound?"

I shrugged and looked to Bas and Finarr. Both bobbed their heads, then all three guys said, "yes," at the same time.

I took the bark plate from Finarr and scooped up some of the mix with my fingers. "At least it smells good. I have no idea how badly this might hurt you, so in advance, I'm sorry."

Violet waved her good arm through the air. "It can't possibly hurt any worse than it already does, and if it keeps me from getting infected, I'm all for it."

I pulled the shirt open then turned to Aislinn. "Can you hold this away from her skin for me?"

Aislinn grabbed the fabric in two places and held it out

and away from Violet's body. It was then that I noticed the red streaks were leading to a tattoo of sorts. I'd never seen anything like it. When an infection spread, it did so in a uniform pattern. Not in a way that looked like a bird on fire.

I suppose I might see flames because of the redness and swelling. I moved closer to her then further away. My vision had been iffy at best, and I couldn't be sure of what I was seeing. It could just be lousy eyesight playing tricks on me.

I honestly had no idea and shifted my focus to the fact that it was spreading far too close to her heart for my comfort. The bird of fire was above her left breast. Thankfully, it wasn't much bigger than a key lime.

Speaking of. I would kill for a slice of key lime pie right now. If I had a marker, I would draw a border around the redness to see if it grew. I decided to use what I had and spread some of the poultice over her shoulder and lower to cover the red areas.

Violet sighed when the sticky paste hit her skin and opened her eyes. "That didn't hurt at all. It's soothing."

"Good. That's good. Do you think you can continue? We've been here a while and need to keep walking. Can you guys find us someplace to hide? We could all use some downtime, but not out in the open like this." I directed my questions to the guys since they were the only ones that knew the realm.

Argies tugged off his shirt and flexed his chest muscles. "My dragon can find the closest cave. That'll be safer and ensure no one can sneak up behind us."

Aislinn and Violet's eyes were bugging out of their skulls as they stared at Argies. If I hadn't seen Sebastian naked, I might have looked too. Fortunately, I had, and now no one else could hold a candle to him.

That's not to say I didn't look and appreciate his well-muscled chest. I was a woman, after all. It would have been impossible not to notice that.

"You could shift behind the trees." Sebastian's voice cracked through the air, followed by a sharp crack that set my teeth on edge.

Argies grumbled and stomped off. "Party pooper," Aislinn told Sebastian.

Violet laughed along with the rest of us. "Some of us wouldn't have minded seeing all that on display."

I shook my head and twisted my torso from side to side to work out the kinks while Argies shifted and took to the air. Based on the rustling in the canopy, I thought he was flying above the treetops.

I saw a bright yellow orb hanging from branches above my head and pointed to it. "What's that? Is it edible?"

Violet's head snapped up while Aislinn looked in the direction I thought Argies went. Sebastian jumped and caught a limb above us, then pulled himself up and grabbed what I hoped was an apple.

He jumped down and sent dust flying when he landed with a smile on his face. "This is *juxule*. It's like an apple. You'll love it."

Aislinn groaned and turned to us. "Is there any more?"

"Yep. The fruit will be higher up. We will toss some down," Sebastian replied before he jumped to the branch and started climbing. Finarr joined him a second later.

Eyeing the fruit, I wiped it off on my shirt then bit into the firm flesh. I'm not ashamed to admit I moaned loudly. Sebastian's head poked through the branches and pinned me with a heated stare.

My cheeks flamed, and I handed Violet the fruit. "It's the best apple I've ever tasted." Violet took a bite, nodding and moaning, as well. Aislinn's hands shot out, and her fingers were curling and extending in a 'gimme' motion.

Violet handed it over at the same time Bas called out a warning.

The fruit dropped afoot to my right, and I darted to catch it. Finarr called out when I had barely noticed the first. I turned to see it floating to Violet's hand. "Use your elements to retrieve them. It's easier."

"I didn't know you could wield the elements like us." Aislinn and I had used the elements many times, but Violet never had. She called upon the power of them to aid in her magic.

"I haven't before. I tried to cast a net to catch what the guys dropped and called on the air to aid me. It sent the fruit toward me instead of Aislinn, who was poised to catch it." Violet removed her backpack and dropped the fruit inside.

"Maybe your powers are expanding in this realm," Aislinn suggested as she waved her finger through the air, stopping the plummet of the next piece of fruit.

I touched my necklace, feeling for the crack that had formed last time I was there, only to encounter a raised design. When I lifted it, I noticed the amber seemed like it melted with the metal. There was now a pentagram surrounded by decorative knots. I didn't know what the changes meant, but I loved each version of the amulet.

Violet shrugged her shoulders and directed more her way as they fell. "It's possible. Who knows? I feel the same. Well, that's not true. My arms hurt like a mother, and I'm exhausted, so not exactly normal."

I dropped the charm and helped with the retrieval while pondering the situation. A couple dozen apples later, Sebastian and Finarr jumped from the tree and took a piece of fruit.

"*Juxule*!" Argies called out as he returned. He was fully dressed when he joined us, much to Aislinn and Violet's disappointment. "Thank the Gods for this lucky find."

"Did you find somewhere we can hide?" I had caught my breath over the last few minutes because I didn't have to continually keep the portal tethered to me. That took more of a toll than I realized.

Argies took a big bite of his apple and bobbed his head. "About five minutes to the east, there's a cave at the base of a small mountain. It's not a straight shot, but it won't take us too long."

"Was that a five-minute flight?" Aislinn asked with a raised eyebrow.

"Umm." Argies swallowed his bite and wiped his mouth with the back of his hand. "Yeah, I was flying."

Violet rolled her eyes. "And how does that translate to walking?"

Argies finished off his fruit then tossed the core into the bushes. "I guess it'll take about a half-hour or so. There's a small hill to climb before we reach it."

That wasn't so bad. I zipped my backpack but left my water bladder out because it was almost empty. "Alright. Was there a creek or anything along the way? We are going to need more water soon." I held up the plastic pouch and shook it.

Argies rubbed a hand over the back of his neck and glanced to the left. I assumed he was looking east and trying to recall what lay in our path. "I didn't notice anything, but I can go back out and search for something."

Sebastian shook his head. "No. I'd rather get there so we can lie down, then you can search for freshwater. That way, we won't be out in the open. It's about time for us to run across those assholes again."

I hadn't been paying attention to how often we encountered the soldiers, but it had been a bit. I was hopeful we weren't going to run into anymore. Perhaps I shouldn't have been so quick to embrace the idea.

I wondered if I could use my elements to bring water to us. I'd have to try that once we got to the cave. It would allow us all to rest. Picking my pack up, I slung it onto my back and engaged air to float the portal again.

As the day had droned on, the weight of the stone archway had become heavier and heavier. Now it felt like a ton of bricks on my shoulders as I tugged it alongside me. I couldn't wait until I could release this burden.

I refused to leave it here, where Fae would have to travel far and through the potentially treacherous ground to get there. The whole idea of me taking it with us was to make it easier for them to access Earth.

## CHAPTER 11

"We've been walking for two hours. Are you sure we're going in the right direction?" This time it was Sebastian questioning Argies.

The dragon glared at Bas. "I know how to tell where I'm going. We haven't been walking as fast as I assumed we would."

I tried to reach out to soothe Bas but ended up stumbling. Sebastian scooped me up and cradled me close. It caught me off guard, and I lost control of the portal. It crashed into a hundred-foot-tall tree. A loud snap told me the trunk had snapped. I waited for the sound of an impact with the ground, but it never came.

I slapped at Bas's shoulder. "Put me down, dammit."

He grumbled under his breath and set me on my feet. I looked at the tree and thought it was leaning on two trees. Only it wasn't. Aislinn had her hand up and pointed in that direction.

I immediately called up my air and lifted the portal. She heaved a sigh of relief then lowered the tree to the forest floor. "That was close."

"I'd say that was more like lighting the bat signal and throwing it into the air so the soldiers can find us," Violet countered as she continued walking. She was cradling her arm a bit less, and her coloring was improving. I hadn't checked the wound yet, but I was hopeful.

The anxiety in Violet's words bled through to me and had my feet moving. I didn't get very far before I had to readjust my hold on the portal and refresh the connection I'd made to it.

"I wish I could take this burden for you." Sebastian's gruff voice explained why he snapped at Argies. He was worried about me. That, more than anything, touched me. He was having a hard time because he had to let me fend for myself while he stood by and watched.

Bas was an alpha male and did things on his terms in his way. There was no give to him. He didn't even smile all that often. And yet, with me, he set what he wanted aside to give me what I needed.

"I would let you take it if I could. The portal is my heritage, my birthright. And it's heavy as hell. Not that I'm carrying the actual weight."

Violet scoffed. "It's not as easy to use air as you're making it out to be. Catching those *juxule* with air was no different than catching them with my hands, except I didn't drop them."

The portal wavered from side to side as if to prove her point. The weight was suddenly lifted, and I gasped then threw out my arms like I was taking flight. Air tightened around the stone along with my gut.

Sebastian smiled at me. "I might not be able to carry it, but I can help."

I laughed at that and lowered my arms. "I wish we'd thought of that hours ago. Hey. I was wondering if you could do something for me when we get home."

"Sure. What do you need?" Agreeing to help me without asking what I wanted him to do was even more proof that he hadn't been lying to get into my pants before.

"My closest friend in my previous life called before we left. From what I can tell, she will be starting over soon, and I'd like you to make her a dragonfly charm. A symbol of the change she will be going through. I can't be there for her in person like she was when my husband died, but I can at least offer this."

Sebastian wrapped an arm around my shoulders while we walked. "I'd be more than happy to do that for you. You've never talked about the death of your husband before."

"It's not something I like to talk about. Tim was the love of my life, and I was devastated when he died. I didn't think I would ever truly be happy again."

I knew I hit a nerve when I said that because he stiffened beside me. I owed him so much. I couldn't give him everything he wanted to hear. "Until I moved here. And I never thought I could love again until I met you. Now I know it's possible."

Bas stopped me and cupped my cheeks. Before he could kiss me, Argies's voice cut through the quiet afternoon. "We're here. Let's get inside before we are discovered."

I laughed and pressed my lips lightly to his, then turned and continued before he could deepen it. Argies was right. Fifteen steps up the rise and I saw the darkened opening.

My shoulders sagged. Crap. The portal wasn't going to fit in with us. Violet clapped my shoulder. "Set it outside. It's not like anyone can come along and steal the thing."

"Right." Fae could carry it with air like I had, but they couldn't move it. Grams and I were the only ones that could. Well, possibly my children. I had never seen any hint they carried magic and wondered if they had any.

After setting it against the mountain, I ducked inside the

cave. We didn't go very far. The cave was only about twenty feet deep, without any other entrances or exits. I sank down next to Aislinn and removed my backpack.

When Sebastian came in, I offered him an apple. I couldn't even think of the Fae name. It was a mouthful. He accepted it and took a seat close to me. Argies set his bag down and moved to leave the cave.

"Wait," I called out. "We can try to bring water to us. We have some power over the elements, right?"

"Why didn't I think of that earlier?" Argies sank to the ground with a groan.

Finarr joined him. "Because few of us go around playing with elements, and even fewer are out in the wilderness where we don't have access to running water and food."

"Ri…" Whatever Argies was going to say was cut off when we heard footsteps outside.

I swear we all held our breaths as we stared at the entrance. I didn't hear the telltale pattern of horse's hooves or the chatter of hundreds of men. It could have been an animal, but none of us were willing to take the chance that we were wrong.

"What the hell is that? I swear if Vodor has done something to my house." The voice was gravel over rocks. Sebastian seemed to relax beside me a split second before a small man entered the cave. He was carrying an ax over one shoulder and a log under the other.

"Who the hell are you guys? And why are you in my cave?" A short, stalky figure was silhouetted in the entrance. I couldn't see anything in precise detail aside from the fact that he was almost as wide as he was tall.

Argies climbed to his feet. "Thursouk, is that you?"

"Argies? Where the hell have you been? And who did you bring into my home?"

Argies gestured to us. I pushed myself to my feet with

great effort. I hadn't been sitting for more than five minutes, and every aching joint in my body was objecting to the movement. "This is Fiona, Violet, and Aislinn, and you know Finarr and Sebastian."

"Is one of these women the hybrid that has pissed off the King?"

Argies looked back at me, where I stood frozen in place. I wasn't convinced this creature meant us no harm. "I'm not sure what you've heard, but Fiona was here before, and she brought her friends to help us overthrow Vodor."

"Your parents will be glad to hear it. The rebellion has been gearing up while Vodor has been decompensating." Thursouk moved through the cave and lit one candle after another, allowing me to get a look around me. What I had assumed was an empty cavern was actually a decent home.

There was a fire ring set in a cove off to one side. There were a short table and cabinets along with fruit and what looked like a skinned carcass. Another indented section had a palette of blankets and pillows. We had settled in what I assumed was the living room of the home.

Sebastian hadn't stood up but leaned forward with one knee bent and his arm resting on top of it. "What do you mean he's decompensating. What's been happening?"

The dwarf paused and met Bas's gaze. "He's been on a rampage for a week since the Queen left. Rumor is that she finally left him for you, and he's pissed. Some are also saying something happened to her, and he lost her power. The worst part of it is the constant stream of creatures he's forcing into the castle so he can drain their power."

My heart started racing, and my gut knotted up. I'd known it was highly likely that he was hurting Fae here, but hearing it made it hit home. "It's my fault. I'm so sorry."

Every head in the room shot my direction. Bas got up and got in my face. "None of this is your fault. Vodor is responsible for being a jackass. All you did was fight back when you were attacked. You shouldn't feel bad about killing Thelvienne for one second."

"Did you say she killed Thelvienne?" Thursouk had inserted himself between us.

I glanced down at the dwarf with his thick red hair, mustache, and beard. I swear his four-foot frame was vibrating as his dark eyes stared up at me. "She was trying to kill me! I didn't mean to kill her, and I never wanted anyone to pay for what I did."

Thursouk scurried over to the bedroom and picked up a battle-ax. His arms were short but muscular. His legs too. He twirled the two-bladed weapon in the air and danced back over. "Rumors are right. You're the one that's going to set us free. We need to get to the Underground."

His happy steps stopped before he made it very far when rocks fell from the ceiling and hit his head. I glanced up like that was going to do me any good. I automatically ducked and lifted a hand to shield my eyes from falling dirt.

"What is it?" My whisper seemed to echo throughout the quiet cave.

Sebastian leaned closer to me. "I think it's more sentries."

My heart dropped to my feet. These fuckers were pissing me right the hell off. "How did they find us?"

"With you tugging the portal behind you, I bet you haven't bothered to shield it or yourself." Sebastian's hands smoothed over my shoulders as he spoke, but it didn't help ease my mind one bit.

I wanted to smack myself. How could I have left such a crucial piece unchecked? Of course, Vodor had my energy signature now. "We need to get the hell out of here. None of us are in any shape to fight right now." Plus, we had to get the portal to a safe location before the soldiers caught up with us and destroyed the stone. I had no idea what that would do to me.

"You have about five minutes before they see you leaving," Thursouk announced.

That got us all moving in a flash. I extended my hand to Violet and helped her up. The second we were outside, I called my magic and noted each of our locations, as well as the portal. "*Caveatis Porcina.*"

With us camouflaged from the soldiers, I hefted the portal with air, and we took off as fast as we could without making too much noise. Within minutes we were far enough away that Sebastian thought it was safe, and we were running again.

Sweat was pouring down my face and stinging my eyes which made me miss the roots. I face-planted in a spectacular display of ineptitude. My poor eyesight wasn't helping matters either. Spitting out the mouthful of dirt trying to suffocate me, I groaned when I heard the crack of the portal slam into a tree.

Sebastian helped with his control over air, but he had to have gotten distracted when I fell. That was going to alert the soldiers as to where we were. I pushed to my feet, barely took a second to float the stone archway before I took off running again.

Everyone else had stopped and rushed to catch up with us. "I'm so sorry," I called out to them. "I didn't see the tree roots."

"I am so sick of running," Violet grumbled. I agreed whole-heartedly but couldn't respond. I had a stitch in my side, and I was breathing through cotton.

Over the past six months I had gotten in better shape, but I was still a middle-aged, out-of-shape woman with a bad knee. How the hell long was it going to take until I didn't feel like I'd run a marathon and was being asked to do a second before I even crossed the finish line?

We'd run an additional fifteen minutes when I slowed down and clutched my side. "I've gotta slow down. I can't keep up this pace."

"I could kiss your feet." Aislinn was sucking in air, and it made her words come out rushed and slightly breathless.

Sebastian kept pace beside me. "We never refilled your water. Here, drink this." With a flick of his wrist, a stream of water headed toward me. I stopped walking and opened my mouth, then took in a mouthful. He went to move the liquid when it splashed in my face.

"Keep it on me, so it washes some of the sweat away." I needed to drink more and be cooled off. "After you give Aislinn and Violet some, that is." I felt like a selfish hag for only thinking of myself.

"We've got them, right Finarr?"

"Yep. We need to be fast, though."

Sebastian moved the water back my way, and I greedily gulped several more mouthfuls when something hit me from behind. It was like I was moving in slow motion. I stumbled forward, and my hands shot out in front of me to break my fall.

I saw the tree from the corner of my eye before it hit my head then my hands slammed into the ground. It didn't hurt at first, and I wondered if I'd been wrong about what had happened.

The pain hit a second later, confirming I had slammed into an unforgiving object. My head spun, and nausea churned in my gut, but I didn't have time to wallow or keep wondering what had hit me.

I heard the sound of fighting all around me. I wobbled as I pushed myself off the ground. A soldier loomed over me, and I urged the air I still had holding the portal to blow faster and move the stone, so it hit the back of the Fae's head.

To my horror, his skull exploded in a shower of bones, blood, and brains. It was freaking nasty. My stomach churned faster, and the bile burned the back of my throat. The world was a green and brown blur for several seconds. Feet shuffled past and sent dirt flying into my face.

I crawled forward and out of the way. "*Sana*," I murmured, trying to heal my head enough that I could fight back. My energy sizzled then vanished. When a body headed toward me, I tossed out an offensive spell to no effect. Groping around me, I found a stick and lifted it when the soldier was on top of me.

When nothing happened, I pulled myself up and pushed with all my weight behind me. The wood punctured the soldier, and he dropped to his knees. Violet screamed from somewhere to my right. My vision danced and blurred when I swiveled my head to look for her. Not moving an inch, I prodded my scalp. I might have had a concussion.

"*Segmentum*." That was Violet's voice casting. A scream echoed right as the dizziness vanished. She had almost cut the asshole in half.

I turned my head slowly to find everyone else fighting soldiers and one of the creeps trying to sneak up behind Argies. Using a tree next to me, I stood up and searched for the stick I had. I had impaled one of the elves we were fighting.

I nudged him in the side. When he didn't move, I yanked it from his body and hobble-ran toward Argies. I wasn't going to make it, so I tried another spell. The weight of the portal weighed me down. It was taking a lot to keep it afloat along while fighting and trying to cast spells. Releasing the archway, it dropped heavily to the ground taking the weight with it.

"*Segmentum*!" The scream left my throat as I concentrated through the pounding in my skull on the soldier lifting a sword above Argies's head. My spell hit him, and blood splattered inside my open mouth from a few feet away.

Argies whirled around, and his eyes went wide when he looked at the two sides spilling guts on the ground behind him. With his attention on me, the elf he'd been battling took advantage and stabbed him in the side with a dagger.

I tried to cast a spell to hit the guy, but nothing happened. When I looked at my river, I found it nearly dried out. Turned out hauling a God-only-knows-how-heavy stone for hundreds of miles really took it out of you.

It didn't help that my previous injuries never fully healed. There weren't many more soldiers facing off with us, so I turned around and headed for Violet to make sure she was okay. The sound of clomping hooves stopped me in my tracks. *C'mon. We just need a freaking break.*

The sound got louder behind me. Before I could turn around, something hit the same side of my head that had become intimately familiar with the tree trunk. The impact felt like the same exact spot. There was no delay in the pain this time.

It knocked me down and made me throw up the apple I'd eaten in the cave. I heard voices but couldn't concentrate on them or decipher what was said. When energy slammed into my chest and made my blood boil, I knew it was a spell.

I heard a loud roar that made me think of Sebastian. I turned my head and saw Bas tearing the soldiers apart. Flames danced on Violet and Aislinn's arms before they tossed them at the body parts. I was going to pass out, but first, I need to make sure my energy signature and the portal were hidden.

I had to take several deep breaths and close my eyes

before I felt the enchantment snap into place. Familiar arms wound around me before I was lifted into the air. “Bas.”

“Shhh. I’ve got you, and I’ll lift the portal.” That was all I needed to hear from him. What remained of my adrenalin vanished, and I sagged in his arms.

When I was jolted a second later, I opened my eyes to see him jump on the back of one of the horses. He had me, and I couldn’t do much more if I wanted to keep the spell cloaking me and tethering the portal to me. Before the darkness took me under, I noticed the river flowing freely. At least my magic rebounded fast.

# CHAPTER 12

"We're about five minutes from the Underground." Argies's voice jolted me to awareness.

I nearly wept with joy. Lifting my body off the horse's neck where I'd been laying was more difficult than trying to bench press an empty bar. Glancing back, I saw Sebastian's smile first before I noticed the bruises marring his gorgeous face.

Turning to the side, I saw Violet sitting in front of Finarr and Aislinn with Argies. Everyone looked like they'd been in a nuclear blast and running for days. The reality wasn't far off. I smelled like a sewer and was covered in dirt and grime. I would be seeing Sebastian's parents again, and I should care, but I had no more forks to give. Let them judge.

I was focusing on what mattered. Things had changed between Sebastian and me. We were getting closer, and I needed to decide what I wanted with him if anything. He wanted to be with me, although I hadn't let him tell me what that meant. This time in my life was about focusing on myself, not a relationship. So, I didn't realize things shifted slowly between us.

He wasn't pressuring me for anything. I created every ounce of stress and turmoil racing through my mind. Why the hell did I do that to myself? Not everything needed to be figured out and labeled. My problem was I didn't do well with ambiguity, and it wasn't in my nature to just roll with life. I liked to think things through and know where I stood with people.

Before I knew it, we were stopping in a tiny clearing surrounded by trees, and I could once again put this off. Sebastian hopped down, then reached up and helped me get off the horse. His hands-on my sides send arousal through my overly exhausted body, and I decided to force myself to simply enjoy the moment without trying to force a decision from my taxed brain.

"Stop thinking so hard. I'm here and not going anywhere. We will tackle this one step at a time as a team. All of us," Bas murmured before pressing his lips to mine. I knew what he hadn't said out loud. He included everyone in the Backside of Forty in that 'team.'

Bobbing my head, I turned with him as he settled the stone archway on the ground. "Are you going to bury it again? Or leave it in the open?"

I considered his question. My immediate response was to hide it underground. Instead, I held my tongue and contemplated the best course of action. It would be better for all if it remained above ground. Vodor wouldn't be in power for much longer if I had anything to say about it. Still, he was right now, and I needed to make sure he couldn't take out the rebellion's power hitter at the worst possible moment.

"I'm going to conceal it for now, but it will have a place of prominence once Vodor is ousted from the throne."

Violet spun in a circle with her head tilted back. "I think

we can dress it up and hide it in plain sight, so you won't have to move a boatload of dirt and shove it underground."

"Perfect. But how?" My head felt disconnected, and light like it was going to float away any second. I had little doubt that I had a concussion. My mouth watered like I was going to throw up again, and there was an insistent pounding in my skull.

"Will it be safe here?" Aislinn asked as she ran a hand down the side of one of the horses.

"I have no idea. It was the only logical place I could think of. What do you think, Argies?" Aislinn's question was like a facepalm. I felt like an idiot for hot having thought of that before.

Argies shrugged his shoulders. "Only those in the rebellion know about the entrance near here, so this should be perfectly safe."

"So, not many people will wander through here then." That was good. I hadn't heard anyone since we stopped, but I assumed that was because it was late.

I had no idea how long we had been riding, but the moon was high in the sky now, so it had to be the middle of the night. Of course, there was every chance in the world I was wrong about that. Time moved differently in Eidothea. Even the daytime hours didn't pass like they did at home.

"This is not along a well-traveled path," Argies confirmed. "This is a back entrance to the Underground, so it's even more hidden. We don't disclose this exit until we are certain we can trust new members."

A breeze blew through the area, followed by a noise in the trees to the left. All heads moved in that direction. I wished my vision was better than maybe I could see more than a couple feet into the trees.

I silently took a step closer to Violet. The crunch of a leaf when I set my foot down made me cringe and go still. Sebastian put a finger to his lips. I nodded in acknowledgment while double-checking I was cloaking my energy signature along with the portal.

It had slipped my mind when I first woke up. It would be just my luck to have lost hold of that and revealed our location. Not only would I land us in a heap of crap again, but I would be bringing trouble to the Underground. I didn't want to lure the soldiers close to the safe haven.

My heart slowed, and I breathed a sigh of relief when I found the spell actively humming away in the back of my mind. When I cast the enchantment, I pictured glue in my mind to ensure it didn't slip away when I passed out—score one for me. Maybe I was getting the hang of this magic after all.

Sebastian and Finarr crossed the clearing on silent feet, making me jealous. How the heck did big oafs like them manage not to make a noise. It made no sense to me. I had lifted my foot with care and placed it down slowly and carefully while they were moving at a clipped pace.

Finarr disappeared behind a tree to the right while Sebastian slid between two evergreens to the left. I met Violet then Aislinn's gaze finding my fear-laced fatigue reflected back to me.

A loud scream pierced the air sending my feet into motion. There was no way I would make more noise than whoever they had discovered in the trees. I didn't hear the beat of horse's hooves in the distance, so I doubted we were facing a large contingent.

I reached Violet's side simultaneously as Aislinn, then paused before we continued after Finarr and Bass. The tone wasn't deep enough to be one of the soldiers. Fae men were far more varied than humans, and their voices along with it. It could be a soldier, but I doubted it.

The sound of Sebastian talking to someone in the

distance eased me even more, and my hands unfurled at my sides. Argies stood in front of us, giving me a perfect view of the smile that spread across his face.

He was walking to the side of the clearing rapidly. He was met at the edge by Finarr, Sebastian, and a familiar wood nymph. My feet were carrying me forward before I could stop myself. The movement increased my nausea and headache but didn't diminish my joy.

"Danalise! What are you doing out here?" I embraced her when they reached me. My steps had slowed, and I hadn't made it very far after all.

"I've been making my way here ever since word started spreading that you had returned. You're back to help us, aren't you?" Danalise's eyes traveled from me to over my shoulder.

Turning, Violet and Aislinn were right behind me. "Violet, Aislinn, this is Danalise. She's a friend of Theamise's. She's the reason I survived my first trip to Eidothea. If she hadn't found me, I don't think I would have survived."

Danalise lowered her head, and she nibbled her lower lip before releasing it. "I'm not so sure about that. You could have beat them. You're stronger than you give yourself credit for."

I put my hand on her shoulder and squeezed. "I might have managed to survive for a bit, but I knew nothing about life here and who to trust or not. I would likely have walked into the castle and Vodor's hands."

Sebastian knelt next to the portal where he had laid it on the ground. "We need to find a way to make this stand up then have you guys do your magic to mask it' presence."

"Will it bring danger to the Underground? I don't want to leave it here if there's a chance to lead Vodor and his soldiers to the area. I couldn't live with myself if he found the rebellion and killed them." I would continue hauling the stone behind me before putting them at an even greater risk.

Danalise bent over and ran a hand over some of the carvings on the portal. "I assume you're talking about this. What is it?"

"It's the object that anchors the portal to Earth. It was buried where the portal used to be. Because of my connection to it, I was able to tether it to me and drag it with us so Vodor couldn't use it to do any more harm."

Danalise gasped. "I had no idea. I can't sense the magic anywhere around us."

I smiled at the proof my spell was working. "That's because I cast a spell to cloak my energy along with the portal. Once we anchor the stone here, I will need to do something else to conceal its presence because it won't be tethered to me anymore."

"Make it feel like a wood nymph. No one would investigate further. Our kind isn't that powerful, and we pose no threat to Vodor. Besides, it will read as any other location in the realm." I looked at Danalise and wanted to hug the woman. Her suggestion was brilliant.

Argies clapped his hands. "That will work. First, we need to secure the archway before we can go any further. Let's lift it to standing so we can evaluate how to keep it upright."

I left Sebastian and the others to get the stone standing. My throat burned with bile, and my head pounded insistently. Before long, the arch stood twenty feet into the sky. It was as wide as it was tall, with each leg placed five feet from the trees on the sides. But it was skinny. Barely five feet thick, so it wouldn't stand up on its own.

"We need braces on each side of the legs," Sebastian pointed out. "If I had my forge with me, I could create some triangles to brace it."

Finarr circled the portal and scanned the structure. "We

can use stone. As long as we locate boulders big enough, we can carve them to act in the same way. It's the only thing we can find quickly."

I bobbed my head then winced when it increased the pain. "We should split up. It'll make it much faster to find what we need."

Sebastian linked his fingers with mine. "Don't go far. The sun will be up soon, and patrols will increase."

I followed Bas, holding his hand, but had to let go within a few seconds. I couldn't keep up. "You go on. Violet and I will keep searching closer to the clearing. My head is only going to halt your progress."

He stared at me for several tense seconds. "Don't go too far. I will be pissed if you get yourself hurt."

I chuckled then saluted him. "I'll try my best."

With a shake of his head, he took off, and I turned to Violet. "Let's see what we can find."

Violet held up her elbow. It was far more movement than she'd be able to manage thus far. "I won't be able to carry anything."

"How is it feeling? I should have checked on it sooner to make sure the infection isn't getting any worse."

She waved me away as I reached for the bandage. "I haven't looked at it yet, but it feels much better. I'm not shivering anymore, and I'm not hot to the touch. Whatever that paste was, it did the job. Let's get this handled so we can find a shower. Please tell me they have hot water in this Underground place."

I lifted my shoulders. "I'm not sure, actually. From what I saw last time, it's like a town down there. There were businesses and cafes and alleys, from what I recall."

"If they've got that, they must have some way to clean themselves, even if it's just a bathtub. Hey, do you think this one's big enough?" Violet was gesturing with her chin to a boulder between two trees.

When we stopped beside it, I guessed it was about five feet tall. It was slightly shorter than my five-foot-five-inches. "I didn't study physics, but I would say it needs to be taller to prevent the stone from tipping forward or backward. I doubt we will find one tall enough, so let's haul it back. We can stack them."

"I'm getting better at making air do what I want," Violet shared as I conjured the element. With a wave of my hand, I had the air wrap around the boulder before gesturing up. I felt Violet's energy mingle with mine in a complimentary if playful way. We hadn't gone far, so we didn't have to maneuver between too many obstacles.

We moved it next to one of the legs and returned to the forest when the others returned, doing the same thing we had. Nearly a dozen car-sized rocks littered the area.

Sebastian scanned me from head to toe for several seconds. His hot gaze made my blood sing and my skin tingle. God, that man was dangerous for my health. Getting dizzy, I braced myself against the portal. I watched as he and Aislinn manipulated the largest boulders to both sides of one leg. At the same time, Finarr and Argies did the other.

"I think you'll need to stack them," I called out.

"That's the plan. Perhaps you should bond them to the archway, as well. It'll add magical glue to the mix," Sebastian suggested.

"That along with anchoring the portal here should secure it in place." I cast the anchor while they placed the supports then bonded them together. It didn't take much energy, but it did make the dizziness worse.

Bracing myself on the stone archway, I tried to cast the mask. "Can you two join me in making it feel like a wood nymph?" Violet and Aislinn both bobbed their heads and joined me in the middle of the arch while Danalise stood off to the side beaming. I sensed her pride in playing a role in the process. I doubted she got involved in much.

Violet, Aislinn, and I joined hands, and I reminded them to keep the image of Theamise and Danalise in their minds. "*Acidis imitantur vitea*." The second the words left our mouths, energy left our hands and encircled the stone before sinking into it.

Sebastian scooped me up before I could protest, and I decided to let him. My head was spinning, and my mouth was watering again. I didn't have to do everything on my own. The first step in changing how I reacted was to allow him to carry me into the Underground.

It was a challenge not to dissect my reaction and try to figure out the reasoning behind it. My mind battled silently for a minute before I closed my eyes and laid my head against Bas's shoulder.

# CHAPTER 13

My eyes flew open when the cool breeze suddenly cut off. I was comfortable in Sebastian's arms but needed to get down. I wasn't entirely certain of the reception we would receive.

I patted his chest to get his attention. "I can walk. My head is better now."

Bas stopped walking and glanced down at me. His expression was shuttered, and he was closed off entirely. "If you're sure. You looked a little green around the gills back there."

"That last encounter with Fodor's soldiers left me with a concussion. It'll heal soon enough." I looked around as we continued down the hall.

The path sloped down sharply, reminding me we were heading below ground. I had never been afraid of being surrounded by dirt and rocks, and I wasn't now either. My heart had to be racing because I was anxious about having the weight of the entire realm on my shoulders.

Violet turned to face me. "Should we keep you awake? Isn't that the proper course for a head injury?"

"That's only if there's a concern there's an intracranial hematoma or brain bleed. It's why we advise people to wake someone after a head injury every two to three hours. If there is a bleed, they will have symptoms like slurred speech, blown pupils, or an inability to be roused. Getting help right away, if that happens, will save a person's life. I don't have any of that, so we don't have to worry."

Violet sighed and shifted her shoulders. "Thank the Gods. That's one worry off the list." It was good to see her injured shoulder moving. Not like the other, but she was able to move the joint. And the bandage wasn't soaked with blood—all good signs.

"Maybe the fates are on our side after all. How is there electricity down here, anyway?" Aislinn was pointing to one of the sconces lining the walls.

They weren't like anything we had on Earth. The light was bright enough that it was impossible to see it didn't come from a lightbulb. Argies had explained they were spells to me. The Fae blacksmiths designed a silver base to tether the light on and hung them where the light was needed.

There was a back panel with a shelf at the bottom. The designs of the rear panel varied greatly. The ones in the Underground weren't intricate like Argies had in his house. They were silver rectangles with short posts sticking out from the top and bottom. Rings hung from the poles, and a circle was welded to them. The light sat inside the middle of that.

Finarr chuckled and shook his head. "We have no electricity in Eidothea. It doesn't work with the magical energy permeating the realm."

"How about indoor plumbing? Fiona and I talked about running water, which I can live without as long as I have a way to wash. But I cannot go to the bathroom in a bucket or something." Violet's face screwed up in apparent disgust.

"We don't have plumbing like you think of it," Finarr replied. "We do use ceramic pots, but they are enchanted to dispose of the waste."

"As long as I don't have to empty them, I can deal with that." Violet shuddered as she continued down the path.

I couldn't help but agree with her reaction. I hadn't thought about the Underground and its amenities. Argies had something similar to a toilet in his house. The last time I had been here, I was running and hiding in the forest and relieving myself while hovering over a hole in the ground. I'd blocked out most of that time from my mind.

We reached a juncture, and I was surprised to see doors lining the halls in both directions. "Where's the main cavern area from here?"

Sebastian urged me to the right with an arm around my shoulders. "It's in the opposite direction. The Underground is set up like a small town, only the streets are tunnels."

I watched the doors pass for a couple seconds. "What's behind there?" I gestured to a wood panel on the right.

Argies passed between us and walked ahead. "They're homes."

I knew some Fae lived down here, but I assumed they were housed in the main cavern buildings. "How many people live down here?"

"I've been gone, so I don't know current numbers. Many still reside in their homes up top. It keeps Vodor's men from hunting too hard for those that have disappeared altogether. Most assume they didn't survive being drained by Vodor," Finarr explained.

"Here we are." Argies pushed open a blue panel and ushered us inside.

My eyes roamed all over the room and settled on the large wooden table and the individuals seated around it. Kelvhan, Eliyen, Teagan, and Chasianna had their gazes frozen on Sebastian and his hands where they rested on my shoulders. I looked around for an exit. I hated being the focus of anyone's attention.

I really should have cared about the fact that I looked worse than something the cat dragged in. I didn't need to do a casual whiff of my armpit to know I was rank. "Hello, again. Good to see you all."

Sebastian's sister, Chasianna, glared at me. "You've created a big fucking mess for us to deal with."

Eliyen, Bas's mom, put her hand on his sister's shoulder. "We agreed to listen to the explanation about the increased attacks."

Sebastian stepped around me and acted as a shield between his family and me. "Enough. You have no right or reason to talk to Fiona like that. You're lucky she's here to help win a war that has nothing to do with her."

I couldn't come between him and his family. I knew some issues had nothing to do with me, but I certainly didn't want to add tension. "It's alright, Bas." I moved to stand by his side. "I will not apologize for killing Thelvienne. She was killing Fae in Cottlehill Wilds and tried to take my head. She left me no choice."

Sebastian's brother, Teague, shared a look with their father, Kelvhan, who focused his intimidating stare on me. "You killed the Fae Queen? A hybrid isn't powerful enough."

There was nothing that pissed me off more than being underestimated. I snarled and took a step forward with Violet and Aislinn at my back. "I could destroy you in the most beautiful way possible and prove to you why storms on Earth are named after people. Bottom line, I'm no ordinary Fae-witch."

"And she doesn't have to be here listening to people judge her," Violet added.

Aislinn crossed her arms over her chest. "Why are we here with these ungrateful cretins?"

"Because they're my family, and they lead the rebellion." Sebastian's words landed like bombs dropped from airplanes.

"Your family?" Aislinn's voice sounded like air being let out of a balloon.

"Yes," I interjected. "We're on the same side, you know."

Argies stepped forward. "Kelvhan, she really did kill the Queen. I witnessed it with my own eyes. She's shielding her signature, which is why you can't sense her power level."

Sebastian's mother stood up and gestured to the empty chairs. "Sounds like we need to be updated. Why don't you all have a seat."

I eyed the blue couch on the other side of the room. It was calling my name. Dirt and grime-covered me, and my hair was tangled. Shower then couch. There wasn't a part of me that wanted to do anything else, let alone deal with the doubt and hatred I felt flowing from these people.

"Is there a restroom? I need to get cleaned up before I have this conversation." It probably wasn't wise to push my luck, but there was only so much a girl could do. And looking like the scum, they thought I was didn't helping my self-esteem.

"We have bathing pools here." Bas grabbed my hand and tugged me through the room and toward a hallway.

I then looked around us and noticed the kitchen area behind Sebastian's parents, complete with a wood-burning oven and a box where they kept food fresh. The décor was simple and reminded me of Argies's home, colorful and comfortable.

We passed two open archways. Glancing inside, I saw the beds. One was covered in a purple blanket, while red covered the other. They looked like mattresses, but I couldn't be sure until I looked closely.

Sebastian stopped at the first door and pushed it open. I never would have called the chamber I entered a bathroom. There was a pool set into the floor of one side with steam rising off the water. There was a mirror on the back of the door and a table along one wall. The chamber pot was attached to a chair that had no seat in the middle.

"I can help clean you," Bas offered.

I laughed and smacked his shoulder. "That will only lead to me getting dirtier. Besides, there is no way I can fool around with your parents in the other room. I won't belong."

"Alright. If you insist." Sebastian lowered his head and took my mouth in a scorching kiss. His lips pressed to mine, making me momentarily forget about his family being close by. His hands knew precisely how to touch me to tease me into a frenzy while his mouth made my need burn through my groin. I tingled and ached for so much more from him.

Pushing against his chest, I broke away. I stared into his gorgeous brown eyes while I caught my breath. "I'm positive. I won't belong. Wait, where's the soap and a towel? I have clothes in my backpack to put on, but nothing to clean with."

"I'd be happy to clean you. And I'm fairly sure we can create enough heat to dry you in a flash."

A groan left me, and a shiver traveled down my back. "You make saying no really difficult. I really want to get cleaned so we can crawl into bed and get some rest." My head was getting better and would be fine after a good night's sleep. I was relieved that the nausea was much better, and the dizziness had been forgotten the second I saw his family and had yet to return. I prayed it wouldn't.

"The soap is here," Bas handed me a flower from the table, then bent and reached back. When he stood up, he gave me a towel. It wasn't terry cloth-like ours. Instead, it was a big piece of fabric. Fae cloth was soft as silk and felt great against my skin.

"I'll meet you out there when you're done. And I'll fill my parents in while you're cleaning up."

I went on my tiptoes and kissed him briefly. "Thank you."

I stripped my clothes off the second he left the room and dropped them in a pile next to the pool. I sat on the stone floor and dropped my legs in the water. Surprisingly enough, it felt like a hot bath.

I braced myself as I jumped in the water because I had no idea how deep it was. I landed with a jolt and ended up waist-deep in the hot bath. The landing hurt my bad knee and reminded me my hips weren't spring chickens anymore.

I knelt down and ducked beneath the water. It felt good to scrub my hands over my scalp and face. When I came up for air, I already felt better. I'd forgotten the flower, so I had to hop out and grab it. The air was cold compared to the water and had me running full tilt for the table.

Plant in hand, I was back inside the bath. The water soothed all the aches and pains from the fights and running through the forest. I looked at the red petals in my hand, wondering what to do. I had never washed with anything like this, so I decided to scrub it over my arms first.

The water made a sudsy film form on the plant. The bubbles increased as I rubbed it all over my body before moving it to my hair. I quickly lathered the locks and dropped the plant on top of my dirty clothes. Dunking my head beneath the surface, I ran my hands through it to rinse the soap.

Before I got out, I brought my shirt into the pool, scrubbed the plant over it, and cleaned it as best as possible. I repeated the process with my pants, socks, and underwear. I would need to find a place to dry them, but they were clean for now, and that was all that mattered. When I got out and wrapped the towel around my shoulders, the urge to sink into a soft bed returned.

No time for that now. I dried off, got dressed, put my boots back on, and laid my clothes out on the table then headed out to the living room. Conversation stopped when I returned, making me self-conscious.

"Ais, Vi, can you guys help me redo the spell hiding my energy? I think I scrubbed it away in the bath, and I'd like you two to add additional layers that will make it impossible for Vodor to locate me." I wasn't taking any chances. Sebastian's parents wouldn't hesitate to blame me if anything happened.

Aislinn jumped up, and so did Violet. "Sure. I'd be happy to help before I take my turn in the bath," Aislinn replied.

We linked hands, and each of us cast a spell to cloak my magic with me going first. Aislinn headed for the bathroom, and I untied the bandage around Violet's shoulder. When I did a check of my river, I found it flowing freely.

If I had so much available, why was I so freaking tired? I should have been able to infuse myself with energy. As I was doing a mental check, I noticed a film surrounding the power. That was another layer blocking access. And it was always there, telling me that I must automatically erect this shield. Probably from years of living with a spell cutting me off from everything magical about me.

When the bandage was unwound, I handed it to Violet and pulled her shirt away from the area. Then I scraped the hardened paste off her skin. "The wound is completely closed. There's a red scar, but it's not open, and the swelling is gone. It isn't infected anymore." Thankfully Violet's back was to the others when I lowered the front edge.

I brushed off the paste I used to cover the redness that had spread toward her heart. The streak that extended from the wound down her chest was gone, but the flaming bird was still there. It was no longer swollen and hot to the touch.

"It feels close to normal. Only lingering pain when I try to lift my arm." Violet bent her arm and lifted the elbow a few inches before she stopped. "I'm going to wait for Aislinn to be done so I can bathe next. Thank you." After hugging me, she left the room, leaving me no choice but to join the group at the table.

Bas gestured to the table. "There's food. You need to eat something."

Aware of the eyes on me, I took the empty seat next to him and scooted it closer to him before looking over the selections. Most of it looked familiar to me from the night I was at Argies's house. I hadn't tasted much that time, and what I did I didn't like.

I ended up picking what looked like the meat he'd given me last time and took a small bite. When the flavor exploded over my tongue, I popped the rest of the piece in my mouth.

Finarr poured blue liquid from a bottle into a glass and pushed it toward me. "It's called *zullon,* and it tastes like wine."

I brought the cup to my nose and sniffed. It smelled sweet, almost like raspberry. My eyes went wide when I took a sip. "This is delicious. I assume Sebastian caught you guys up. What can I share to prove I'm on your side?" I tackled the issue head-on rather than trying to avoid it anymore.

I had gotten lucky with Tim's parents. They loved me and treated me like a daughter. The more I ate and drank, the better I felt. My eyes were no longer in danger of slipping closed.

Sebastian's sister watched me closely. It was unnerving as hell. "They've told us some pretty unbelievable things about you moving a portal that has been in the same location for millennia. First, you claim to have killed the second most powerful Fae in Eidothea and then the portal."

"Chasianna." Bas's voice held a warning that promised untold pain and suffering.

"It's okay, Sebastian. They don't have to believe us. As long as the others are willing to join us in our fight against Vodor."

Argies sat forward and tapped the table. "We need to spread the word about the portal being located in the field close to the back entrance."

Sebastian nodded and handed me another piece of meat. "And tell them it will feel like a wood nymph to them. Do you think your grandmother will let the most vulnerable through?"

My head felt better. The pain had decreased, making it easier to follow the conversation. "Absolutely. Should we send them through before we make a move?"

"I'm not sure that's wise. I'm afraid it will tip off Vodor and give him time to prepare for our attack. Or it could cause him to lash out even worse than he already has," Argies interjected.

"Enough. We will not be sending Fae to the middle of nowhere where they might walk into a trap," Bas's father barked.

Something in me snapped right then. I pushed to my feet, sending my chair clattering to the floor behind me. "I don't give a shit what you think. I'm sorry you're too small to realize a hybrid has more power than a full-blooded Fae. I have put my life on the line for your people, and you have yet to say thank you. If you think any of this has been easy, you're wrong. Although it was easier to kill the Queen than it was to move the damn portal."

Eliyen put her hand on his dad's arm. It stopped him from snarling back at me, I'm sure. "The portal was harder to move because it shouldn't have been possible for a half-breed. I don't recall the prophecy indicating the half-breed would out-power our kind. Perhaps we need to have another look at it."

"Let her go home," Teague, Bas's brother, replied. "We don't need her and don't need to consult some damn prophecy."

"On that, we can agree. It doesn't matter what some elusive seer said, however long ago. All that matters right now is that we pool our resources to beat Vodor. You can waste your time and energy doubting me and my abilities if you'd like. I'm getting some rest. And there's an easy way to verify I am telling the truth. Go up to the field and knock on the portal. My Grams will answer."

"With luck, Isidora will help them pull their heads out of their asses," Aislinn interjected as she returned to the room.

Kelvhan stood up and extended his hand to me. "It's hard to erase thousands of years of thinking." I accepted his hand, expecting him to shake it. He didn't do that; he laid the other one over it, and I felt his energy surround me then sink into my skin.

The atmosphere lightened in that instant. I would tell them anything they needed to hear to keep their hope up. Believing they had a chance would go a long way to making us successful. If warriors already thought they were defeated, they would fall before they even began.

# CHAPTER 14

"Are you sure this is a good idea? Your parents didn't exactly roll out the red carpet for us." I refused to keep my mouth shut when I worried what traipsing around the Underground on Bas's arm would bring our way.

I ended up sharing the bed with Aislinn and Violet. None of us wanted to separate and relocate to other homes in the Underground. I was acutely aware of his parents trying to convince him to remain in Eidothea after removing Vodor. I know his dad wanted him to take the throne. There was no way I would ever stand in his way, but part of me prayed he would return to Pymm's Pondside with me.

My gut had been in knots for hours, and my mind was a whirlwind. It was entirely possible I would be going home without Sebastian only to find my Grams gone, as well. At least I would have my bitches by my side.

"My parents do not reflect the feelings of the realm. Word has spread about how you killed Thelvienne and people wanted to catch a glimpse of the powerful hybrid." Sebastian's gaze was full of pride when it landed on me.

I rolled my eyes and tried to hide the heat that built in my cheeks. All embarrassment was forgotten a second later when we entered the underground city's main cavern. We had been walking through a maze of tunnels that had magical sconces and colorful wooden doors.

Nothing stood out much until we reached this area. Now, I understood why we hadn't run across anyone else. They were all milling around the shops down here. The noise level went from our barely heard footsteps to hundreds, if not more, voices all talking simultaneously. It was a lot to take in. I had to stop at the mouth of the tunnel and take everything in.

I hadn't gotten a good look the first time I had visited. Now, I saw one- and two-story stone buildings set up in a square with concentric squares outside of that. There were at least four layers before reaching the core grouping of shops in the center. Like the halls of homes, the doors on these structures were just as colorful.

Unlike the residential section, there were stained glass windows, signs, and various other items decorating outside this area. One shop had flowers painted on the windows and walls. Another had birds and other creatures painted on it.

"Is that her?" My head whirled around when I heard the whisper-yelled question. A tall, slim elf woman was leaning toward a shorter, curvier elf woman. I had no idea which one had spoken, but it had to be them. They were both staring at me.

I grabbed Bas's hand and tried to melt into his side and disappear. I wanted to pull him back when he took a step forward. It made others stop around us. Before I knew it, several conversations erupted, all centered around my identity.

"You sure do know how to grab attention, don't you, Fi?" I glared at Violet, who was behind us with Finarr. Aislinn and Argies were still back at home. I had discovered it belonged to Finarr.

"How do you know they aren't staring at you? You're the one with the big boobs."

She laughed at me and tugged her shirt down. "They are a sight, aren't they?"

"Hey, Adriana. Yes, this is Fiona and her friend Violet," Finarr interjected in response to the elf women.

The taller one beamed at him and clapped her hands. "Is it true? Did she really kill the Queen?"

Sebastian growled low in his throat, making them jump. I smacked his arm. This time he ignored my attempts to calm him. "Yes. Fiona obliterated Thelvienne. She will be respected as the powerful Fae-witch she is. You don't want to get on her bad side."

"Don't," I whispered to him.

He cupped my cheek and ran a thumb across my lips. "You will not be treated poorly here. You deserve their undying devotion for what you've already done for them, and they should never forget that for one second. Besides, power and strength is the only thing Fae kind will respond to."

I decided to trust him and ignore any further questions. "You promised me the best meat pies in Eidothea."

Violet poked her head between us. "Don't forget about the Fae version of cupcakes. I want to try those!"

Sebastian chuckled and led us down a street between buildings. We passed by several stores. One looked like a grocery store, another looked like it carried tea, but it could have been dried herbs. All I could say for sure was that they had barrels of dried plants.

In the second square of shops, all I could see were the ones closest to us because some shops cut off our view of the other side. "That looks like the place Argies took me to get clothes last time. The fabric here is the softest you've ever touched, Violet. We will have to visit one of them soon."

"I'd love that. When we aren't in the middle of planning a war," Violet replied with more excitement than she'd had since crossing the portal.

Her shoulder was healed entirely this morning. It could have been the afternoon because we had no concept of time down here. While the scar was nothing more than a thin pink line, the flaming bird was still on her chest. None of us understood, but it wasn't causing her problems, so we put that off to figure out another time. I personally thought it was kinda like my amulet—a change from crossing the portal.

"How do you guys stay safe and hidden down here?" Violet's question brought me out of my head. I had missed some of the conversation and was surprised to see we were now in the middle of the downtown Underground.

The center of the shops contained a stunning garden. How the heck did they have grass and flowers without any sunlight? Given the pixies flitting around the park-like area, I guessed it was thanks to their magic.

"The Underground was created shortly after Vodor took the throne. Every creature in the realm knew immediately he was corrupt and would be bad for survival. Hence, they started creating this location," Sebastian explained.

Finarr waved a hand around them. "The first buildings were created right here in this central square so Fae could shop freely without fear of being taken to the castle while they were out and about. Some dwarfs dug out the first homes for victims to take refuge. As the atrocities grew, so did the Underground. And here we are today. Our population here rivals that of Midshield."

"To answer your question, Violet. The Underground is hidden and protected by a collective barrier the King and his men cannot find." Sebastian pulled me toward a group of stalls set off to the right while he spoke.

I had been so focused on looking at the stalls they had in this section I hadn't noticed the stares being sent our way. There were too many Fae to count, and they all seemed to be focused on us.

I wanted to check out the ceramics offered at one of the stalls but didn't dare ask Sebastian. It would only draw more attention to us. He continued walking and ignoring all the onlookers. He headed straight for a stall set up outside what looked like a restaurant.

There was an outside seating area with tables. The door was a deep purple color, and the plate glass window had what looked like a pie with steam coming off of it painted on it.

"Torvo! It's good to see you again." Sebastian embraced the Fae.

Torvo held Bas at arm's length, then looked over at me. "It's about time you pay me a visit. I heard you were here not that long ago, and you didn't stop by. I'd be offended if I hadn't heard what your companion has been up to."

Sebastian chuckled and wrapped his arm around my shoulders. "This is Fiona. Fiona, this is a good friend, Torvo. He and his mate make the best meat pies in the realm."

"So, the rumors are true? You killed Thelvienne?" Torvo directed his question to me while he did something behind his counter. He opened something that was either holding or cooking food because steam and a spicy, herb-scented aroma lifted in front of him, making my mouth water.

I walked closer and peered over the edge to see him grabbing what looked like a pot pie from beneath a stone lid that he'd lifted. He put it inside a ceramic bowl and scooped a ladle of gravy from a pot set to the side of the opening with the pies.

"That looks delicious." Heat filled my cheeks when I realized I had been so focused on what he was doing I had ignored his query. "To answer your question, yes, I killed her. It wasn't intentional. I was fighting her and didn't realize how powerful my spell and fire were. I'm not sorry. I just think it's important to point out I'm not some homicidal maniac."

Torvo titled his head to the side and considered me. "I have no idea what that means, but you've done more than the rebellion has managed over the last century to improve morale. For the first time, we have hope we will be out from under Vodor's evil thumb soon."

Torvo handed me a bowl with a spoon, then gave one to Bas, Finarr, and Violet. "It's on the house." The Fae waved Finarr's money.

I shoved my spoon into the flaky crust and inhaled the savory scent and steam that was released from the food. My mouth watered as I shoveled the first bite into my mouth. A groan left me, and my eyes rolled back in my head. "This is delicious. I haven't found much food that I like in the realm, but I could eat this every day. So good."

Violet made similar sounds and gestured with her spoon. "We need to get this recipe. I'd like to try and make this for the kids."

Torvo's chest puffed up, and a broad smile broke out across his face. "It's a family secret, but I'll happily share it with our saviors."

My next bite stuck in my throat, and I nearly sucked it down the wrong pipe. The tightness in my chest was worse than heartburn. Sebastian clapped his friend on the back. "We will be back by another time. The council is waiting for us to join them. I'll have Teague drop the bowls off later, as well. Perhaps you and your mate can join us for a meal soon."

Torvo nodded and started making a bowl for the Fae

standing behind us. No one was pushing for him to hurry. They all seemed to be listening to our conversation. Thanks to the countless conversations going on around us, I wasn't able to hear what anyone thought.

Sebastian gestured with his utensil in the opposite direction we'd come from. I kept pace beside him, eating the pie as we walked. Violet almost ran into my back when Bas stopped in front of the largest building in the main square. I hadn't seen the entire downtown Underground, as I thought of it, so I didn't know if it was the largest overall.

Finarr opened the green door and held it wide. Bas entered, and Violet and I followed. The entrance was open and had chairs set along one wall. Double doors were propped open along the far-left.

When we looked inside, I was surprised to see Aislinn and Argies seated at the massive table on the other side of the room. Chairs were set up in a stadium-style seating in a fan between us and the table. At least a dozen others were sitting with them, including Sebastian's parents.

I was very self-conscious when all eyes shifted to us upon entering. At least we weren't the only ones that had food there. The food was too good not to finish, and I didn't have enough to offer the others. My Grams and parents had raised me to always offer others a refreshment.

Sebastian's father stood up and pinned us with a look I couldn't interpret. "You're right on time. We were just about to discuss the best approach to the final battle in this war with Vodor."

Sebastian set his bowl in front of an empty seat next to Argies and held the chair next to his out for me. "I told you we were on our way." I sat in the chair and noticed Violet sit next to Aislinn. I wished I was next to my friends. The Backside of Forty made a formidable force when we were together.

"I see you grabbed the best meat pies in Eidothea," a Fae woman pointed out. I couldn't recall her name, but I recognized her from the first time I spoke with this group. "Torvo's cooking is nothing short of magical. Now that we're all here, shall we get right to the point? We need a plan of attack."

Kelvhan nodded his head once in response and took his seat. "We need to hide our presence throughout Midshield during the day. As soon as night falls, we will spread out and surround the entire palace. We will need to move into position carefully so we don't alert the guards before everyone is in place. Once everyone is in place, we will sneak into the castle in the middle of the night. It's the best times because patrols are fewer then."

"It will help if there is a distraction. Otherwise, so many of us maneuvering around the city will be noticed." I had no idea what the guy's name was, but he wore a scowl much like Bas's father did.

Finarr shook his head. "Something that would gather the guard's attention would be suspect in and of itself. Activity in Midshield s far too orderly for such an event not to draw scrutiny."

"That's the idea." Kelvhan set his fork down and set his fists on the table. Was he trying to intimidate us? "We want them to focus on, let's say, an argument and not on visitors or the surrounding areas."

I rolled my eyes and swallowed the bite I'd been chewing. "We're on the same side here. There's no reason to get into a pissing match. Acting out of the norm will backfire and cost lives. Vodor won't only focus on the event in question. He will expect it is a diversion, and knowing him, quadruple patrols."

Several people started talking at once. The noise in the room rose with each passing second. I sat there eating my meal while I watched the discussion. Sebastian began yelling at one point before he glanced my way and shut his mouth.

"They aren't going to listen, Bas. At this point, it would be a better idea if we made a move on our own. I want to live through this fight, and these assholes are too concerned that their position is the right one to see reason." It wasn't until I paused to allow him to respond that I realized the room had gone quiet.

I swear a pin could drop in the silence. My gaze skittered around, never staying on anyone for very long. Some were obviously pissed, while others were shocked. Whatever. I didn't need to be a soldier to know a stupid idea when I heard it.

Aislinn finally broke the silence with a chuckle. "Fiona is right, but for those of you that don't like her or are too biased to see her strength, I ask this. Why go with the loud approach when stealth works just as well? Why is it necessary to make that much noise? If you're looking for credit for the plan, you need to check yourself. That is a very Vodor way of thinking. It doesn't matter who proposed what. The idea is to overthrow him with the least number of casualties as possible, right?"

Sebastian's dad glanced from her to Bas, then me before he finally nodded. "Fair point. I suppose there's no reason not to go in quietly."

"And we can take out guards one by one, replacing them with our men. It will be much easier if no one suspects anything is amiss to remove them without being detected." That came from the first lady to talk after we arrived. Everyone seemed to like that idea.

After that, others tossed out ideas. They all centered around surrounding the palace without being detected before moving on the King and his men. We needed to maneuver as many of our own soldiers into position before infiltrating Vodor's walls. Once we were on his territory, we were in his hands. No one knew if he had traps or anything else staged around the palace.

I finished the meat pie and leaned back in my chair, giving an opinion when I thought it was necessary. I could do much more. An earthquake rumbled through my insides, and my heart was trying to take flight right out of my chest. This was really happening. I needed to gear up before we made a move. The jeans and t-shirts weren't going to cut it.

# CHAPTER 15

"Are you sure it's smart that we go to the surface to get this gear? It feels too risky." Aislinn's question was valid, and I considered the truth to her words and looked to Finarr and Teague. Sebastian's brother had joined Teague to escort them to the clothing shop in the Underground.

Unfortunately, they didn't have the materials necessary to create the clothing the three of them needed. Ever since she had visited the first time, they'd been making combat gear for countless Fae that wanted to join them in the fight, so they were out of supplies.

Finarr clapped Aislinn on her shoulder. "There's a risk just being here. It's minimal. The guards lost track of us long ago, and there will be no reason to suspect us going shopping for clothes. Besides, I've known Midurri my entire life. She's the second-best clothing maker in all of Eidothea and keeps the lined fabric for combat gear in stock. She's one of us, even if she doesn't live down here."

Teague glared at us. "Go into battle without the proper protection. Why should we care or put our lives on the line?"

I really wanted to throat punch Sebastian's little brother. "Why are you with us, anyway?"

Teague stepped close to my face. "Because Finarr is my best friend, and I will not leave him to supervise the three of you."

Finarr stepped in and pushed Teague back away from me. "Tensions are high, I get that, but we can't start fighting amongst ourselves. We're all here to overthrow Vodor. Now, let's get them outfitted and get back before the meeting ends."

*You can kick Teague's ass. You have more power in your little finger.* The thought was reassuring because it was true. Ever since I came back here, I noticed I could sense the energy surrounding everyone—even Violet and Aislinn.

I had a feeling it had something to do with the changes in me, as reflected in my amulet. For lack of a better description, Sebastian's aura was the brightest and strongest aside from Aislinn. Violet was just as vibrant but in different ways. Her signature wasn't like the Fae. That had to be thanks to her witchy heritage. Teague and Sebastian's parents weren't exactly dull, but they weren't as strong as my friends, either.

"We'll be fine, Ais. Don't forget the Backside of Forty can kick some serious ass. There's no one here to rival our strength." My words were the truth and earned me scowls and grumbling from Teague.

Finarr laughed and walked to the exit Bas had shown me the day before. He wanted us to know how to get out of the Underground if there was an emergency. The ascension was quick, and before I knew it, we were outside in the exact location I had entered the first time I visited.

A brisk wind blew through the trees. The sun was high in the sky but did nothing to erase the chill in the air. The colors here were far more vibrant than were found on Earth. And the air was sweet. There was no pollution.

"It's so quiet here," Violet observed as she spun in a circle and looked around. "I have never considered how much noise pollution surrounds us even in Cottlehill Wilds."

Aislinn's head bobbed up and down as Finarr lead the way. "Remember when we went to London? The trains, busses, and airplanes overhead added a deafening level of sound. It's a wonder we managed to beat those dark Fae back."

"I used to live and work close to a city. I never thought about the commotion that always surrounded me until I moved to Pymm's Pondside. That was a harder adjustment than discovering I had magic." I had never considered that before and couldn't help but wonder what that said about Earth and how humans lived.

Violet turned to walk backward as she replied. "That had more to do with going from a house with three kids to an empty one. I should know. Now that the twins are gone, I'm more than a bit lost. The silence is the cherry on top of a shit sundae."

I knew exactly what she meant. "You'll find your purpose. I hope it doesn't involve moving to a new country like I did, but you will always have the Backside of Forty even if it does. Thank God they invented FaceTime calls. That way, you won't even miss Aislinn's stunning smile."

Aislinn snorted. "This is just a bump in the road. What's important to focus on is what truly makes you happy. That's what mid-life crises are all about. Realizing you've spent half of your life working and doing what you're supposed to without much consideration for what makes your heart sing."

Violet turned back around, but not before I saw the mischievous glint in her eye. What was that about? I didn't have to wonder long. "True. And I've noticed a certain dragon makes your heart sing, Ais. I think I heard how long and loud he made you croon last night."

"Wait." I held up my hand with a chuckle. "How the heck did I miss that? I thought she was in bed with us." I never once heard her get up and sneak out of the room.

"If I'm not mistaken, it was during bath time." Violet's tone was teasing.

When I cocked my head to the side, my chuckles turned to laughter when I saw how Aislinn's cheeks were turning pink. Finarr joined in the laughter, but Teague ruined the moment. "We're planning to face our greatest foe, and you guys are worried about sex. Unbelievable."

I shrugged my shoulders, not letting his censure bother me. "Someone's never had a true partner in life. Otherwise, you'd know love or intimacy is what makes all of this worthwhile."

Finarr held up his hand to halt further discussion. "We're getting close to town. We need to be on alert. Just because I said it was safe doesn't mean we can let our guard down."

Finarr's recrimination was enough to make me set aside the scathing "Wait. I don't have any gold or whatever you guys use to pay for things. How are we going to get the gear?"

"Don't worry about that. We have it covered. Like I said, Midurri is on our side," Finarr explained.

I bobbed my head but kept my focus on the structures popping up now. We hadn't passed any other facilities thus far. Now that we were encountering homes, I knew we weren't too far from the town. Argies had told me before that we were close to small cities or towns when we ran into more and more houses.

A few seconds later, voices reached us before we cleared the trees, letting us know we were very close to Steelgate. "This is where you and Sebastian grew up?"

Teague's gaze was elsewhere when he gave me a clipped nod. "It is."

The street here was dirt, but the buildings here were very similar to those built in the Underground. The smell of fresh-baked bread reached us first, followed by savory food and sweets.

Looking into the first large window, I marveled at the leather hanging in the window. I paused for a second then noticed a cobbler making the traditional moccasin-type shoes Fae wore. We passed a bakery a few seconds later.

The sight of loaves of bread made my mouth water. I didn't see any sweets—just various kinds of bread, from dark to light brown. I wondered if they had rye. I loved a good rye with pastrami.

The next shop looked like a candy store. "Is that a lollipop?"

"That looks like divinity," Violet added.

Aislinn pressed her face to the window. "Can we go in here? Is there any chocolate?"

Finarr shook his head. "No time. Midurri's shop is right here." I followed Finarr's finger to see him pointing to a shop across the street.

We were on the shop's stone porch across the street when I noticed Teague wasn't with us. I glanced back to see him leaning against a wall with his arms crossed over his chest. "Is he coming?"

"He's keeping watch from there. I'll be inside," Finarr assured us. That was actually a relief. I didn't need to have Sebastian's brother watching me be fitted for clothes. He didn't like me to begin with.

"Midurri!" Finarr's voice made me turn back around to see he had opened the door and entered the store.

We followed him inside, and I wasn't surprised to find a centaur staring at us. Midurri was tall like her sister, at least seven-feet. Her hair was dark brown, unlike her sister. They did have the same hazel eyes.

Aislinn and Violet were staring at her with their jaws on their chests. We passed the wire mannequins with clothes on display in the windows while more hung on hooks along the walls.

Midurri smiled at Finarr behind the long wooden table while her front legs stomped the ground several times. "Good to see you're back, Finarr. What brings you in today?"

Finarr stopped a couple feet from the centaur and maintained a relaxed posture. "I have special friends that need battle gear, and I promised them you are just the person to outfit them."

Midurri's eyes flared, then shifted from him to me, Aislinn and Violet. I knew she couldn't feel my energy. I'd learned the first time I had visited Eidothea. Thankfully, I didn't need to take one of the potions like last time. I'd already masked my presence.

"Is she the hybrid that came through the portal? The one that killed the Queen?"

"She is. We are going to make a move, and they need to be protected. Will you help?"

"Of course. Come with me." Like her sister, she felt that was enough to get us moving and trotted to the back of the store. I grabbed Violet and tugged her. She snatched Aislinn's hand before we made it more than two steps.

Before we made it to the arch, Midurri had disappeared in the back. There were bolts of fabric and piles of clothing in the back area. The centaur was motioning us forward. "Here, put these on. Quickly."

"Thank you," I replied before shucking my pants and sweatshirt. Unlike her sister, she didn't leave to allow me to change. Sensing their discomfort, I nodded to Aislinn and

Violet. After stuffing my legs into the dark brown pants, I pulled the shirt over my head.

This fabric was soft yet stiff, unyielding, and big. Midurri motioned me forward. "Let me adjust that for you."

"Thank you for helping us. I already feel less exposed." I held my arms out to my sides and heard my friend gasp when she pulled out the sides of the top before chanting the same word her sister had. She followed suit with the pants, and both items shrank around my body until they were as snug as leggings.

"We all need to do our part. I can't fight, but I can do this much." The centaur grabbed something from the side of us that I couldn't see.

I lifted one leg and tried to bend it. The fabric was stiff, leaving little room to move around. How was I supposed to fight in this? It was better than the alternative. The magic imbued in the fabric made my skin tingle.

"Pretty cool, huh?" I loved almost everything about Eidothea once you took Vodor and his soldiers out of the picture.

Aislinn bobbed her head. "I need to learn that spell. It would make shopping so much easier.

"Your shoes," Midurri ordered. I lifted a foot heard a commotion in the main room. She slipped something on me then picked up my other foot, forcing me to wait to run out front.

Violet was headed to the arch, but Aislinn didn't make it more than a couple steps before Midurri grabbed her and adjusted the clothing. I left them to it and stopped in the middle of the passage between the two sections.

The shop was filled with soldiers, and Finarr was on the ground bleeding profusely from a head wound. "That's her." I gaped at the guard that had outed me. His finger was like a laser-focused on my chest. How the hell did they find us?

"What are you talking about?" I called my magic up and felt flames waver across my knuckles.

"You might be hiding your magic, but your auburn hair is distinctive enough to confirm the reports we received. You're the hybrid that stole something from the King. You aren't getting away with it, either." Spittle flew from the guard's mouth as he spoke.

Where was Teague? I craned my neck to see if I could find him. There was no one standing where he had been before we entered the shop. We were severely outnumbered. I needed to try and take out a few soldiers with my magic.

"I'm not who you think I am. I've never stolen anything in my life." I turned to the side and flicked my wrist, sending a fireball hurling toward the guard.

He laughed and held up an amulet that sucked my spell inside. I didn't see another casting until I heard Violet cry out before she landed in a heap. The side of her gear was smoking.

It hadn't been sized to her body, so I was able to see where the fabric had been eroded. Her skin had a deep purple bruise but didn't have a gaping hole. My heart stopped when she didn't move a muscle.

Aislinn hurried out of the back before I could rush to Violet's side. The soldiers all reacted at once. One threw a spell at me while another hurled a wire body at me, and another tossed something at Aislinn. I wasn't focused on her, so all I saw was something flying through the air from the corner of my eye.

I scanned the street for Teague again but didn't find him. Maybe he went to get Sebastian and Argies, and they would come to our rescue. I needed to buy us some time. I had to be careful to keep my energy hidden. I didn't want to announce my location to the entire realm.

I didn't want to set the shop on fire, so I cast lightning

toward the biggest group of soldiers. The grunts weren't what I was hoping for. I wanted them crying out in pain. They repaid me in kind, and I felt electricity slam into my chest and steal my breath. Then I was airborne for a couple seconds until my body hit the corner of the table.

For a split second, all I could think about was how my lungs refused to expand. Aislinn shouted something I couldn't hear over the noise in the store. Hooves clomped, men screamed, and magic flew around.

I hit the floor with a groan and grabbed my side. I swear it punctured a kidney. There was nothing like flank pain. I rolled away from a boot before it stomped on my skull. I swiveled my leg as I moved and swiped the guard's ankle.

He hit the deck next to me, and I kicked his chest. Movement from the corner of my eye made me turn in time to see a fireball heading right for me. My arms flew up to cover my face and head. The force behind the flames knocked the breath out of me with bruising force.

Hands grabbed under my arms before I gathered my wits. I writhed and wriggled, all while kicking my feet out in an attempt to get free of the guards that had a hold of me. "Not going to work this time." Cold metal clanked over my wrists to punctuate the threat.

I screamed and called on my fire, wanting to burn the hands on my arms. Electricity fizzed in my core then winked out, leaving me cold and empty. I had never felt like this in my life. It was as if someone scooped out my insides during an ex-lap surgery.

I tried again, but nothing responded to my call. I closed my eyes and sought out my river. It left me vulnerable, and I wasn't all that surprised when hands clamped down on my ankles. Splitting my focus was precarious, but I was able to see a thick film covering my river of magic. It wasn't a dry bed, but something was blocking it.

When I heard the baying of a horse, my eyes flipped open. Two soldiers were attacking Midurri. Blood dripped from an injury to her front flank. The sight broke my heart. She had been hurt because I entered her shop.

I renewed my escape attempt. I was bucking like a wild bronco and managed to get one foot free. Pulling that boot back, I kicked it toward the Fae on my left. I connected with a chest but didn't have enough force to stop him. He grabbed my leg before I could wind up again.

Something black descended over my face, cutting off all light. My head went into a grand mal seizure as it jerked and flopped, trying to dislodge the black bag. It was harder to breathe with the thing on. My heart was pounding painfully in my chest.

I tried to pry the goo off my river but couldn't do anything. The black hole in my chest threatened to swallow me whole. I hadn't felt this cut off when I had a spell keeping my magic inaccessible. I had never been so powerless as I was carried away from my friends. I needed to find a way out of this, or I would die a gruesome death at the King's hands.

# CHAPTER 16

Pain exploded in my chest as I was tossed on something hard. With my arms and legs finally free, I bucked and tried to toss myself off whatever I was on. With my feet kicking in the air, I knew I was off the ground, but I had no idea how far up I was. I could be twenty feet in the air, but I didn't care.

It would be better to break a leg than let the king get his hands on me. My palms landed on coarse fur. I had to be on a horse. That was the nudge I needed. Using my arms, I shoved my body backward and into a solid wall of muscle.

"*Non mouent.*" The second the soldier behind me muttered those words, my body stiffened and stopped fighting to get free. The animal surged into motion, throwing me backward again.

Scrawny arms banded around me, caging me in. The energy from the soldier made my skin crawl like bugs were burrowing underneath my skin. The wind whipped my hair back, and I shifted my focus to the cuffs on my wrists. They were rendering me incapable of fighting back.

There was no catch that I could release to pop them off.

The surface had some kind of design engraved on it. My fingers were zapped when I ran them over the markings. I tried to force one of them down and over my hand, but it wouldn't budge. At first, I thought it was because of my thumb, but it didn't move a fraction of an inch. They weren't coming off.

I needed to escape then deal with the cuffs. Rubbing my cheek on my shoulder, I moved the black bag enough to see grass and leaves fly by beneath us. I was definitely on a horse. I could see its front right flank and leg as it galloped.

I stopped fighting. The only way I had a shot was to make the guard think I'd given up. Letting my shoulders slump, I dropped my head. The arms weren't cutting off my air anymore. My body moved side to side with the animal.

Putting more force into each swaying movement, I waited until the right moment. When the soldier's arm lifted from one side, I threw my body in that direction. I threw my hands out but didn't manage to keep from hitting what felt like a tree. The rough bark scraping the side of my neck and the rounded surface clued me in.

My head slammed into the unforgiving surface. My orbital socket had barely healed from the previous injury when it broke for a second time. Swelling immediately closed the orb. I didn't have time to delay.

Nausea churning in my stomach, I crawled away and yanked the bag off as I moved. The light blinded me, but I could see I was in between two trees, and at least half a dozen soldiers were jumping from their horses and yelling to capture me.

The pain was so bad I wasn't sure I could move. To make matters worse, I could only see out of one eye. Yet, somehow, I managed to get to my feet. I swayed and lumbered five feet before two sets of hands grabbed my upper arms with bruising force.

"Nice try. You can't escape us." With that, I was lifted to a soldier who yanked me roughly in front of his body. This time my stomach was draped across the animal, and a rope wound around my ankles.

My head throbbed, and I swear I was going to pass out. I used my energy to stay alert. There was no way to get away at the moment, and I couldn't risk another head injury. I might already have an intracranial hematoma. I certainly didn't need to make matters worse.

Dust choked me when the horses took off, making me cough and suck in some dirt. My aching chest and stomach slammed into the horse's back with each step. It seemed like we rode forever while at the same time didn't seem that long at all. It was the discomfort that prolonged the trip.

The horse hadn't been stopped for even a second before a foot flew toward my face. I lifted my head and was rewarded with a boot to the chin. It dislocated my jaw but saved my eye from being decimated.

I tried to twist mid-air, so I could catch myself. I made it to my side before it impacted with the ground, knocking the wind out of me for the second or third time that day. My body was never going to forgive me for how it was being treated.

I braced myself for the rough treatment as they pulled me to an upright position. I tried to look around, but with only one eye, all I saw was a large grey wall on my good side. There was a door a few feet away and grass leading up to it.

What hit me square in the chest was the dark energy. It was the only way I could think of the suffocating feeling. There was no light in sight. It drained every ounce of hope or joy before I could grasp hold of.

I was going to die here. There was no escaping the soldiers as they shoved me through the door. When the panel slammed behind us, it cut off the sunlight and left little to see by.

We stood in a narrow hallway surrounded by dark grey stone that dripped with brackish liquid and a dirt floor. Noxious fumes hit me a second later. Every ounce of fresh air had been replaced with rot and death.

All sound had cut off, as well. The combination of low lighting, rancid stench, and silence made me feel like I was immersed in a deprivation chamber. It was surprising how rapidly my mind started screaming, and I had to fight the urge to turn and try to run.

Instead, I bent and removed the rope from my ankles. I didn't run my fingers over the sore skin. I had little doubt there were cuts and abrasions, and I didn't want to introduce bacteria into them. I had no way to clean them and keep them from getting infected.

A hand shoved my shoulder, sending me stumbling down the path. The slick feel of the wall beneath my hand when it landed there made the nausea churn even faster. The smell reminded me of kombucha. Not something I liked even a little bit.

The pressure on my chest made it even harder to breathe. Malevolence surrounded me, trying to sink into my soul. It took great effort to keep the corruption at bay. Whatever spell Vodor had on his castle was intense. Within a few feet, the temperature dropped below freezing, and my breaths came out in white clouds in front of my face.

The gear Midurri had sized for me provided some insulation from the cold, but not enough to keep me from shivering. The soldiers prodded me every time I slowed down. I knew they were guiding me to a dungeon.

There was no way this was the main entrance to the palace. Vodor was far too egocentric for that. This was meant to intimidate and instill fear. I had to admit it was working.

I lost more and more hope with each step deeper into the bowels of Vodor's hold. I hadn't realized I had slowed down again until strong hands threw me into the wall. My battered cheek hit the stone.

Dizziness had my head spinning. By the time I managed to clear it enough to continue, I felt warm wetness trickling in a steady stream down my cheek. I cringed at the thought of whatever coated the walls getting in my wound while also thanking God the blood was draining. The pressure in my eye had gotten to the point I could no longer feel it.

That wasn't the case anymore, and I embraced that discomfort. It meant I wasn't in danger of losing it for the second time in as many days. I was pushed down the tunnel more than I walked it. We reached a circular cavern with at least a dozen cells dug into the walls every few feet before long.

In the center of that space was a set of shelves and on those shelves were random objects. I didn't have long to look, but I thought I saw a couple jars, some bones, and a hatchet along with chains and more cuffs like I had on my wrists.

This view confirmed my suspicions. "I see Vodor is into dungeon chic."

That earned me a snarl and a boot to the rear. I flew into a set of bars. "Shut up, bitch."

I braced myself while I sucked in a breath. The clang of metal echoed loudly throughout the room. If you could call the cold, dark cavern a room. "Inside the cell hybrid."

I pushed myself off the bars, but that wasn't fast enough. Two soldiers grabbed my arms and tossed me inside. I stumbled forward with my hands thrust in front of me. There were about three and a half feet of space, so I hit with enough force to make the back of my hand touch my arm.

I collapsed to the dirt and braced my aching head on my

knees. There was nothing inside the cell except what smelled like fecal matter. Dark energy zapped me, making me yelp in surprise. It was the shadow trying to seep into my body. Whatever it was sent, the guards scurrying away.

I hurt too much to wonder about the odd behavior. I was up shit creek without a paddle. I was locked inside Vodor's dungeon with no way to access my magic or get out of there. In short, I was screwed and not in a good way.

My gaze scanned the area around me. Three of the walls were stone, while the one in front of me was comprised of metal bars. I crawled to them and pulled myself up. I was on one foot when the air froze around me.

I couldn't seem to suck in a breath when a tall Fae materialized in the main room right in front of the shelving unit. The black light surrounding him battered at my senses and confirmed he was the elusive Vodor.

He was handsome. Women would no doubt fall at his feet. His short black hair was perfectly styled, and his green eyes glimmered. The smile oozed across his facial features, making my stomach squirm.

"It's nice to finally meet you, Fiona Shakleton. You've made quite the stir in Eidothea."

"That happens when you fight against pure evil." I flexed my fingers and clenched them into fists as I tried and failed to access my magic. That goop was even thicker now.

Vodor tossed his head back and chuckled. "You're full of fire. I owe you a thank you for ridding me of my mate. She was becoming a liability. I had hoped she would follow Sebastian to Earth and stay there, but she was hell-bent on making him suffer and me right along with him."

I rolled my eyes at that. "Based on the tantrum you threw, I know you're lying. I bet it burned to have a weak hybrid like myself kill your mate then beat you at your own game."

Vodor closed the distance to the bars and snarled. His

disgusting attempts at charm vanished to reveal the ugly demon beneath. "Watch yourself, Fiona. You are at my mercy, and most days, I have none."

"You will regret kidnapping me. When I get out of here, I am going to rob you of every ounce of stolen power." It was too freaking easy to goad the greasy Fae.

Vodor shouted and shoved his arm through the bars, extending his finger toward me. He never said a thing, but the next thing I knew, I was on the ground, huddled into a ball.

It felt like every ounce of energy I had was drained in an instant. There was a tug on my soul, and it made my chest hurt like a bitch. My ears started ringing, and my fingers were frozen blocks of flesh and bone. I swear my skin withered dry while Vodor took everything out of me. I was going to die before I had time to contemplate my current condition further.

He had hands of death and destruction. The thought popped into my head, trying to steal every ounce of positive energy I retained.

The suction stopped suddenly with an earsplitting howl. The next thing I knew, I was on the floor in the dark. I was panting, and it took several seconds until my heart settled enough that I could hear anything aside from my breathing.

Vodor had vanished, taking the light with him. My body unclenched, and the cold receded enough, so I was able to move my fingers and toes again. I sat up and positioned my back against the bars, so I avoided the slimy walls.

That was a million times worse than when he had connected to me through the portal while I was on Pymm's Pondside. Based on the way he was howling, I'd say I kept him from getting a damn thing. That made me smile.

I wanted to pat myself on the back for that little win. The sound of tiny scurrying feet distracted me. My head swiveled left then right. That had to be rats or mice. Did they have rodents on Eidothea? They might not be the same as we had on Earth, but there was no doubt there were flea-infested, disease-carrying critters living in this dungeon.

"Ugh!" A full-body shiver rattled the bars and made my stomach turn. The revulsion shifted to cold. I needed to get warm. *What's the point? You're going to die here anyway. Why not die and rob Vodor of the chance to take my power?*

I was grateful Vodor left, but I would freeze to death soon if I didn't do something. I tried to conjure flames, bypassing the blocked canal of my power river. My fingers went to the cuffs, and I tried for the third time to remove them. It was hard not to claw my skin to pieces.

When I ran a finger over the inscriptions, there was a spark. It lit the area directly in front of me and confirmed there were nasty things down here with me. I didn't manage to get a good look, but sharp teeth inside an elongated snout refused to leave my mind.

"Shoo," I called out, kicking out my feet. I had to send these things fleeing. Within seconds I was hyperventilating, and all I could hear were my panicked breaths.

I sat like that for hours, it seemed. Those feet had sharp claws that dug into the skin at my ankles as Fae rats tried to scale me like a mountain. Adrenalin kept my hands and feet moving to brush the fuckers off. My eyes would droop, and the pitter-patter of claws would startle my eyes back open.

My body hurt, and I was certain I was bruised from head to toe. Lethargy weighed down my limbs. It took great effort to keep the beasts away. Throughout it, all my breathing never once slowed. I was pretty sure the sound of those tiny feet would haunt my dreams for the rest of my life. I was light-headed from all the panting.

Light illuminated the hall a second before footsteps made me go still. Soldiers were returning. While I didn't trust what they gave me, I prayed they were bringing water and something to eat. I needed fuel to keep me going. I had been running on adrenalin so long it had tapered off despite my fear spiking once again.

"Hello, bitch. You ready to give the King what he wants?"

"Hmmm. Let's see. Uh, no. Never going to happen." I tried for a mocking tone but wasn't sure I pulled it off.

A flame flew toward me from one of them. It was too dark for me to see who had cast the spell. I hesitated before I ducked. Part of me wanted the flames to warm the chill I was beginning to believe would never leave me.

One of the soldiers stepped into the meager light closest to my cell. His hands went to the waistband of his pants. "I'm going to enjoy this. Saddle up. The rest of you can have a turn next."

Gruff laughter followed. My blood froze in my veins, and my heart dropped to the filthy floor. The clanging of the door echoed the sound my heart made. The panel was opening, and the organ raced faster than a rocket going to the moon.

"*Prohibere*!" My hands flew up, and a string of lightning left my palms and hit the soldier in the groin.

He screamed and fell to his knees while I scrambled to grab hold of my magic. I needed to keep the reins so I could get the heck out of there. Unfortunately, it slipped through my fingers.

"I'm going to make you pay for that. And then I'll take what I want from your battered body." He would have been scarier if he wasn't bent over and speaking through a clenched jaw.

"You wouldn't dare touch the King's prized possession, would you? I'm fairly sure he doesn't take kindly to others playing with his toys."

One of the other guards nudged his shoulder. "She's right.

We shouldn't be doing this. If we caused her any damage, he would rip our heads off."

"Don't think this is over, bitch. As soon as he's done with you, I will be waiting in the wings to finish you off."

My knuckles were white where I clutched the metal bars. I was barely holding myself together. All I wanted to do was fly apart. I tried to muster the energy to fight and find a way out of here but could hardly move. Sebastian was going to save me, right?

The fleeting hope I clung to slipped through my fingers like water. I had never been a negative thinker and always told my kids to see the silver lining. I was surrounded by nothing but death and destruction. Losing hope and giving up wasn't an option, but I couldn't find a shred of anything to cling to at the moment.

Do not give up! Suck it up, buttercup. I hadn't given up when Tim was battling his cancer, and I wouldn't start now.

## CHAPTER 17

Chances were high that Violet and Aislinn were dead. Finarr, as well, for that matter. That thought haunted me more than any other. The last I had seen, they were both injured and unresponsive. I couldn't see enough before I had been dragged out of the shop to know if they were okay.

They had to be alright. I would never forgive myself if I was the reason they were killed. Violet and I had been best friends for longer than I could remember, but Aislinn had come to mean just as much to me. This was not how my magical new beginning was supposed to go.

I sat huddled in the cold with my back against the bars. Thankfully, every sound echoed throughout the dungeon, making it easy for me to detect when someone was headed my way. I had no desire to get more of the slime on my clothing and body than necessary.

My head felt like it was a watermelon that had been split open. Since moving to Pymm's Pondside and accepting the Guardianship, I have had one battle after another with countless injuries. It hadn't hit me until my magic was once again blocked from me that accelerated healing had come along as a perk.

A necessary perk, if I was honest. Having magic put me in the crosshairs of some pretty nasty people. Without the ability to get over my wounds quickly, I would have lost this war before it even began.

It seemed like the Goddess Violet talked about, or one of the Gods Aislinn mentioned was evening out the odds. Until Vodor finally got his hands on me, that is. I had no concept of time in the pitch black of my cell.

All I heard was the pitter-patter of tiny claws of Fae rats all around me. I had gotten one brief glimpse of whatever creatures were down here with me, and they were hideous. Seriously, I would be haunted by their red beady eyes and sharp teeth for the rest of my life.

Of course, that was rivaled by the way the guards insisted on taunting me. They'd returned at least half a dozen times since that first encounter. Unfortunately, I never again felt the crackle of lightning on my fingertips. All I had to do down here was contemplate my doom and evaluate what had happened in search of a weakness and way out of here.

During my endless reflective moments, I concluded that the zap I managed was thanks to sheer terror. I couldn't reproduce it no matter how hard I tried. And none of the subsequent taunts prodded me into action, either.

The guards had been crystal clear about their intentions that first visit. One of them had even unbuttoned his pants, proving how serious he was. There was no way in hell I was going to sit by and become a hapless victim.

Fighting, it seemed, was in my blood. And I will always fight with whatever means I have. It appeared that producing the meager sparks was enough to keep the hungry wolves at bay because they hadn't approached like that again.

That now-familiar scurrying made another shiver run

through me, rattling my back against the bars, only this time it wasn't from the cold. The constant noise kept adrenalin dumping into my system and kept my energy focused on finding a way out of there.

The dungeon's sensory deprivation would have been more frightening if they got rid of the rats and kept the guards away. Without anything to focus on, the despair would seep into your bones, leaving you a sobbing mess.

The throbbing in my eye was yet another distraction from the mess around me. The bleeding had stopped, leaving behind an open wound at risk of infection. I needed to get the hell out of here and find my friends. I had to keep the faith.

Sebastian got to them in time and brought them to safety. Midurri and Finarr, too. I hope he found his brother. I couldn't be sure what happened to him. He might have taken off to get help when he saw the soldiers. Not that it made much sense. Why would he leave us vulnerable and outnumbered?

*He doesn't like you, Fi. He likely can't stand the thought of a woman saving his ass.* Could he have set us up? My gut churned, and an objection immediately sprang to my mind. I couldn't believe he would get rid of any asset in their fight against Vodor. He didn't have to like me to see how I could help their cause.

My fingers ran under the cuffs for the hundredth time. My skin was raw, and I had scratched cuts into my skin. I tried not to create more injuries where I could possibly get an infection, but I couldn't stop. Whatever the bands were, they cut me off from my magic, and that was my best chance of getting out of there.

The sound of footsteps preceded dim lighting by a couple seconds. Seemed like it was time to torment me again. I sighed and swiveled to face the oncoming. The group was far larger this time, and it made my heart skip a beat.

It hadn't started racing yet. This was status quo for the guards, and the more they came, the less their taunting affected me. Not once had they carried a tray with food or a bottle with water. I kept hoping for it each time. I needed something to keep me going.

"To what do I owe the pleasure this time?" Not one of them had anything in their hands. I don't know why I kept hoping they'd at least bring me water. They didn't give a shit about me.

"The King wants to see you." A guard at the front of the group was the one that had spoken. He had to be one of the leaders. Every time he was with the group, he led the discussions.

My head snapped up from where it was resting on my knees. "What did you say?"

"We can do this the easy way or the hard way." He completely ignored my question.

Two of the guards approached the bars and waved a hand over one section. A blue light flashed before a click echoed in the room. I wondered how they unlocked the door since there was no deadbolt securing it. Of course, it was magic. What else would it be?

A third guard pulled the door open, and the leader, along with two others, entered. Instinct made me move away from them. I didn't get very far. The leader grabbed a fist full of my hair and yanked hard enough that I swear he pulled out chunks of my scalp.

The other two guards grabbed under my arms and hauled me toward the door of the cell. "Where are you taking me? You don't want to hurt the King's prized possession, do you?"

The leader snarled at me and leaned down until his face

was in mine. "You will keep your mouth shut and do as you're told."

My heart was beating frantically in my chest, and I couldn't catch my breath. All I could think about was the fact that they were going to rape me, or worse. Immediately I started writhing and fighting their hold. The ones holding me stumbled a couple feet outside my cell.

I was right in front of the shelves, so I kicked out, trying to set them all off-kilter. The unit rocked, and several items crashed to the ground and shattered, but it didn't fall over. The leader approached me as I bucked and fought—his fist connected with my injured cheek.

The only reason my eye didn't explode instantly was that he hit several inches below the throbbing orbital socket. He did manage to stun me for several seconds, and it was all they needed to gain control and have two more grab my ankles.

I didn't stop bucking and pulling at my limbs in an attempt to get free. They carried me down the narrow hall. I assumed it was the same way they brought me, but nothing looked familiar. When the tunnel started climbing, I thought maybe they took a turn, and I missed it. I was convinced we had gone a different way when they carried me through a door I hadn't seen before.

We left the rough stone walls behind and entered a finished section of the palace. While I continued to fight, I cataloged my surroundings. Not that there was much to see —plain beige walls and ceiling. I couldn't see the floor, and so far, we hadn't encountered anything else.

"Put me down. You'll regret it if you hurt me." If Sebastian found them, he would rip them apart.

I might not have been ready to consider the relationship between us. But I knew without a doubt that he'd fallen in love with me and would do anything for me. With my death imminent, I realized I didn't need to do some deep soul searching to know I felt the same way about him. What a fool I'd been.

"I can't wait for the day when the King allows us to have our way with you," the leader replied as he drove a fist into my side. We were in a much wider hall now, and he was able to keep pace at my side.

"I see you're a coward. Hitting a woman when she can't fight back. Pathetic." I probably shouldn't taunt him, but in my experience, men like him lowered their guard when they got pissed. I was hoping to get them to make a mistake.

Voices got louder and louder as we continued down the hall. I was panting and had stopped fighting while agony tore through my side. That fucker had a mean right hook. We passed by a door that seemed to be the source of the noise and continued.

We climbed one set of stairs to another level. Here the walls were pale green, and there were paintings of Vodor in various poses. My entourage stopped outside a room. I heard the panel open, and a feminine voice saying, "Put her in the bathroom."

That made me stop fighting them. I could use a bath. The guards carried me through what looked like a bedroom. When I twisted my head, I saw a large bed covered with a blue blanket. There was a dresser of sorts with butterfly statues and a bust of Vodor. The walls were a darker shade of blue, and there were landscape paintings on the walls. I didn't really get a good look at anything before they carried me through another door.

They stopped in a large room with grey walls, where soft female voices filled the space. I saw a counter with a bowl of water, and when they sat me down, I caught sight of a massive bathtub. It was more like an above-ground pool.

Stairs led to the top, and at least five female elves waiting with various objects in their hands.

They didn't look like much of a threat standing there with their heads lowered and the straps of their pale-yellow slip dress practically falling off their slender shoulders. I wanted to fight my way out of here but knew better. Just because these women looked broken didn't mean they were. Now I was surrounded by a dozen or more of Vodor's loyal subjects. I wasn't taking a chance with my life.

Now that I was out of the dank dungeon, a weight lifted from my chest. I would find a way out of here and be reunited with my friends. All of them were alive and looking for a way to rescue me.

"Get her ready." The leader turned on his heel and was walking out before anyone responded to him. Several of the guards lingered in the doorway.

To my horror, the women started in my direction. My tired heart had slowed when we entered the bathroom. It was now beating much faster. "I see being a nasty pervert is a cross-species thing. I guess I shouldn't blame you, what with your lower intelligence."

One of the guards growled and lifted a hand covered in flames. The leader stepped back inside and clapped him on the shoulder. "Get out of here if you know what's good for you. The King gave explicit instructions she was not to be touched."

Nausea churned in my gut, making me want to vomit. Given that they'd physically carried me out of the dungeon, I suspected what Vodor had been referring to. To my surprise, one of the women set the bowl she was holding down and crossed to the door, then shut it in the guards' faces.

"Keli!" One of the other women hissed. "Don't make them angry. You know how they get, especially Darnell." That was interesting and perhaps something I could use.

"Can you guys help me get out of here? Please. I'm being held against my will, and I need to get back to my friends to make sure they're okay." For the millionth time, I tried to feel them through the connection we'd forged when I shared my power with them to dilute the signature.

Keli shook her head with a frown on her face. "I'm sorry. We can't do that. There is no way we will make it past Darnell and the others. And I will never do anything to risk my family. If one of us goes against the King's orders, he will kill our families while we watch before doing the same to us."

My heart sank. It had been a long shot, but some small part of me had hoped I would be able to convince them. "Can you at least remove these cuffs? I think they cut me off from my magic, right? Without them, I can get myself out of here. I managed to kill Thelvienne. I can break out of the dungeon."

All of the women gasped. "We'd heard rumors she was dead. You must be the hybrid of prophecy. I wish we could free you of these bindings. It would save us all. The King is the only one that can remove them. We don't have much time. We need to get you ready. Take your clothes off, so we can wash you."

I pondered what they said while removing the filthy gear. It wasn't the first time I had heard about a prophecy. Regardless of any prediction, however long ago, I would do what I could to help free the Fae of their oppressive King. Besides, given my current predicament, I doubted it was about me. I was about to die at the hands of Vodor.

Keli led me up the stairs and into the water. The hot liquid immediately soothed me. The groan I let out came from the core of my being. I had been cold and shivering for days for all I knew, and I was covered in dirt and grime.

"Use this to wash your face. You'll want to be careful of that eye. It looks dreadful." Keli winced when she handed me what looked like a loofah. It was closer to the natural sponge than the synthetic ones.

"Do you have any herbs? I can create a paste to make sure it doesn't get infected."

Keli shook her head. "They've only given us soaps to clean you with. All you need to worry about is bathing so we can prepare you for the King."

"Thank you." I didn't bother asking them for anything else. They wouldn't give me anything, anyway. Every time they tried to wash me, I grabbed the soap or oil and did it myself. There was no way I was going to allow them to wash me. It was nearly orgasmic to dunk my head underwater and scrub my hair clean.

I felt like a new woman and was happy to find my determination pretty solid at the moment. Vodor had some awful mojo working to dismantle every ounce of hope I experienced. His choice to attack me mentally was brilliant. It was the only way he had any chance of debilitating me and getting me out of the way.

The towel was fluffy and warm when I stepped out of the tub. I had barely made it down the steps before the women descended on me. They primped and prodded and draped me in a silky red dress. The color always brought out the red in my hair.

While I loved the gown's feel and appreciated the stunning design, I wished they had placed me back in my battle gear. It provided some insulation and shielded me from the grimy dungeon.

The women were brushing my hair and pinning it up while I tried to move my mind away from the ominous message the dress sent. I wasn't going to be returning to the dungeon. Vodor, it seemed, had plans for me.

There was no way to prepare except to reserve all of my

energy to fight him. No way was he going to get his hands on me.

Keli opened the door and ushered me to the outer room. The guards stood at attention all around the space. Darnell grabbed my arm and tugged me to the hall. "Cooperate, and you can walk in of your own accord. Fight us, and we will carry you, exposing your body for everyone to see."

I followed him like an obedient prisoner. The women had taken my underwear, and there were none to replace it. I was entirely too exposed already, as it was. My breasts were far bigger than the Fae women I'd seen this far, and gravity plus age plus children meant they resembled ski slopes. I usually didn't care, but the dress was tight and made it obvious I had nothing on underneath it.

That alone kept me from trying to escape. I didn't want my lady place, as my Grams called her vagina, to be shown to Vodor. No need to prompt him into action. The halls of the palace were busy with staff hustling about. It was impossible to determine what they were doing, and honestly, I didn't care. They weren't going to go out on a limb and help me.

My jaw dropped, and my heart leaped into my throat when Darnell ushered me into what I thought of as the great hall. I read as often as possible in my previous life, and I loved watching historical movies and anything supernatural or magical. Those stories all seemed to have a castle with a great hall.

It was exactly like I always pictured. Massive stained-glass windows lining the walls with tables set off to one side and a dance floor close to a band that was playing music. There were lots of flowers, twinkling lights and a bar with drinks.

There was also a long buffet filled with various foods. My stomach rumbled even while it was churning, and I fought nausea. The King is showing off to his court, she is laughed at, and food is thrown at her.

All eyes shifted my way. I brushed my hands down my gown and tried to stay in place when Darnell shoved me toward the King. I stumbled and fell forward. My hands flew out, and I caught myself on a guy that had been watching me. He pushed me away from him and sneered at me.

I was drug down the aisle to the pair of gold thrones on a dais at the end of the room. Both were gold and covered in engravings with a maroon velvet seat cushion. One of the chairs was smaller than the other and empty. Vodor sat in the bigger one with a bejeweled gold crown on his head.

"As promised, the entertainment for the evening has finally arrived. My eyes flew open, and I was breathing so hard I almost passed out.

"No," I whispered.

Vodor got to his feet and glared down at me. "Shut your mouth and get on your knees." He was pointing to the side of his throne, and before I made a move to comply or tell him off, the guards had thrown me down in roughly the spot he wanted.

My head was spinning, and I glanced around at the well-dressed men and women laughing. There had to be at least fifty people there, and they were all enjoying my humiliation.

Women looked down on me while men vacillated between leering and openly taunting me. "This has to be some mistake. She's far too old to be capable of besting Thelvienne." It was a feminine voice, but I couldn't place who had said it. Old, my ass! I'd like to show her what the word meant.

Her comment spurned the party-goers into action. I was no longer seen as a threat. Men and women alike approached the dais to toss food at me. Before long, I was covered in stinky fruit, meat, and gravy. Something acidic hit my face, making the cut around my eye sting.

Vodor was laughing with a group of guys off to the side while delicious food was wasted. Not wanting them to know how much this was getting to me, I picked the meat off my body and popped it into my mouth. I needed the nourishment.

That didn't last too long as Vodor ordered the guards to hold my arms while his closest friends talked about having a go with me when Vodor had gotten what he wanted from me.

Seemed I wasn't so repulsive after all. I wasn't sure I could survive what he had planned for me. That hope I had found again was withering, and he didn't even need to return me to the dungeon.

# CHAPTER 18

Goop dripped from one earlobe while the silk dress was plastered to my skin. The novelty of tossing food at me had worn off, and I was ignored in favor of dancing. I watched in horror as the party took a decisive turn.

Couples started kissing while they danced. Hands were roaming all over bodies without concern that they were being watched. I didn't think I was a prude or anything, but watching people grope one another was not my idea of a good time.

I wanted to close my eyes but knew that would earn me a boot to the face, so I watched as the event devolved into debauchery. I kept my gaze focused on the food table to avoid seeing too many of the assholes around me.

It seemed like the party lasted for hours. Too damn long to be kneeling on the marble floor while Fae around me had sex and did God only knows what. I hadn't bothered watching, so I couldn't say for sure.

My bad knee was killing me, and my hips were reminding me I wasn't twenty anymore and shouldn't be staying in a position like that for more than five seconds. That was joined by my bladder pipping up for the first time in what felt like days.

I usually got up several times during the night to pee yet hadn't been to the bathroom once since being thrown in the dungeon. I'd been deprived and bordered on dehydration, which was undoubtedly why I hadn't felt the urge before.

Apparently, the bathwater I'd accidentally consumed had already worked its way through me. Being humiliated like this was a whole new experience in torture. My shoulders slumped, and I wanted to lie down. I'd managed to eat a bit of the food thrown on me. It wasn't enough to fuel me, so exhaustion continued to ride me like a Harley on the highway.

My eyes started slipping closed when I was jerked to my feet unexpectedly. Darnell was back with his cohorts, and they were pulling me toward the exit. It was far harder to ignore the disgusting display before me when they were sure to knock me into as many couples in the throes of passion as possible.

I let my eyes go unfocused and listened to the conversations I could catch. Not everyone was having sex. Some were gossiping about Vodor being at the height of his power even without Thelvienne. All because he'd caught another of his long-time enemies and dealt a blow to the rebellion.

That spurred another dump of adrenalin, making my heart race and my mind return to thinking about my friends and their fate. Violet and Aislinn weren't enemies of the King. He didn't even know they existed. Sebastian, his family, and all of the rebellion were person non-grata.

Teague had been at the shop with us. It had to be him that had been caught. I shouldn't want that as badly as I did, but it beat thinking it could be Sebastian. The air-cooled the second we were out in the hall. I hadn't realized how hot it had been in the great hall.

A contingent of guards stood two or more deep, blocking me from the main entrance. At least that was what I assumed the massive double doors were. It made sense. They didn't want me escaping. I didn't outright try to run, but I tried to reaccess my magic. I couldn't reach the river I thought of as my elemental power source. It was still covered in concrete.

I could see blue light rising off the water like steam. Vodor was indeed draining me. While they lead me through the palace, I focused on putting a barrier up so he couldn't take it anymore. It was far more critical to protect myself. There wasn't a way to get away from a dozen highly trained soldiers.

The décor shifted, and the walls turned beige. Then we were through the door and walking through the cold, narrow tunnel. It wasn't until I realized I had no way out now that I managed to erect a barrier between my river and Vodor's spell. I had no idea if it was wishful thinking or not.

I couldn't feel it like I did when I cast protection around myself. And I hadn't used an incantation. Returning to the dungeon ebbed away at the millimeters of progress I'd made toward reclaiming my hope.

I shivered so hard I hit my elbow on the rock wall. It hurt like a mother but quickly vanished. The cold froze the area soon enough. I shook off as much of the food as I could. I didn't want to bring a veritable buffet to the rats.

Someone was bellowing in the distance. Whoever they had captured was in one of the cells and was pissed. I clenched my fists to hide the way my hands trembled. *Keep your shit together, even if it's Sebastian.* That was going to be next to impossible but was vital. They would use my feelings against me if they saw it bothered me.

Several guards in front of me hurried forward and threatened to hurt the other prisoner if they didn't stop trying to break the bars. My heart was in my throat, and I couldn't suck in a full breath. A tight band strangled my chest, trying to take my life along with my hope.

My eyes flared then blurred with tears when I saw who was in the cell next to where they had kept me. I tilted my chin up and bit back the emotion threatening to cut me off at the knees.

"I see you're still killing it with controlling your prisoners. Vodor really should think about replacing you." I prayed they didn't hear the warble in my voice.

Sebastian barked out a laugh. "You always were a pompous jackass, Darnell." How the hell had they gotten ahold of Sebastian?

I closed my eyes for a second, praying that when I opened them, he would be gone. My heart cracked when I saw it was fruitless. He was just as screwed as I was. And he was baiting the guard just like I had.

I was thrown roughly into the cell I had been in before and landed on my hands. The landing wrenched my wrists, but I barely noticed it. Walking around with a broken eye socket twice now made other injuries pale in comparison.

The door clanged shut, and Darnell hurried over to Sebastian's cell with flames on his palm. Before I could open my mouth, he threw the fireball at Bas. I shoved my head through the bars and tried to see if he was okay.

It was difficult to bite my tongue and keep from calling out to him. Knowing we would both suffer more is the only thing that stopped me. I refused to give Darnell and his cronies any more reason to hurt us.

The previous threat came rushing back to my mind. Seeing the animosity between Bas and the guard, I guessed he wouldn't hesitate to rape me in front of Sebastian and lie to Vodor about it.

Darnell laughed as the flames spread across Bas's chest. His shirt hadn't caught fire. I prayed he could get it out before it really hurt him. While my heart was in my throat and I was ready to jump through the bars to help him, Sebastian casually reached up and smothered the flames.

"Get some rest. The King will be in soon to teach you both a lesson," Darnell promised before he and the others turned and left. They didn't extinguish the torches lighting the cavern, so I saw when the Fae rats raced from their hidey-holes.

"Sebastian," I whispered as I craned my head to look at him. "How are you doing? No, *what* are you doing here?"

Bas wrapped his hands around the bars, his chest heaving with his breaths. "I couldn't stay away after they took you."

"Of course, you could. The rebellion needs you. You should have stayed away." There was no way out of this dungeon. Now we were both looking at a death sentence. It was my worst nightmare.

"There was nothing that could have stopped me when Teague told us you had been taken."

I would have done the same thing. There would have been no way to keep from trying to rescue him if our roles had been reversed. "Are you okay? Are Violet and Aislinn? What about Finarr and Midurri?"

I wrapped my arms around my middle, trying to get warm. It was exponentially worse to be standing there with a soiled silk dress on with soft-soled slippers. I was going to die of hypothermia.

"Violet and Aislinn suffered pretty severe head injuries, but one of our healers has treated them. Last I checked, they were recovering very well. They said they couldn't feel you at all, and I lost it. I should have thought it through but couldn't stop myself from attacking the palace."

I lowered my head to the bars. Was he skipping over our

other friends because the news was bad? "I would have done the same thing, I'm sure. Please tell me Finarr and Midurri are alright."

"They're fine. Minor injuries. We need to get out of here and sneak into Vodor's bedroom and kill him in his sleep." Bas ran his hands over his chest, brushing away some ash.

"Wait. How come you weren't burned?"

Sebastian glanced down at his shirt. "I managed to cast some protection before they clamped the restraints on me. I knew they would cut off my ability to use my magic."

I held up my cuffs. "These things are pissing me off..." I stopped talking when I heard footsteps traveling down the hall. It wasn't the loud clomping of the soldiers. It might be more rats coming, but I couldn't be certain.

Keli cast furtive glances around the cavern as she hurried toward my cell. She had something clutched in her hands. She stopped when Sebastian let out a loud growl. I shook my head. "Keli, what are you doing here?"

She held up the parcel in her arms. It looked like my battle gear. I would be indebted to her if she brought my clothes back to me. The soiled dress was sticking to me, and I was beginning to smell awful.

"I can't let you out of there, but I thought you could use these. That dress offers no warmth or protection."

"I could kiss you right now. Thank you so much. I know it was a risk to help me. Listen for an attack and get out of the palace as soon as you hear anything. The rebellion will be making a move soon, and I don't want you caught in the crossfire."

She bobbed her head, handed me clothes through the bars before she turned around, and ran out of there like her ass was on fire. It was good to know not everyone in the palace was on Vodor's side.

"I wish I had some way to wash this filth off me," I

complained as I shucked the silk and stepped into the clean battle gear. My skin was sticky in places and made it hard to get the clothes on.

"What happened to you? How's your vision?" Bas's jaw was clenched, and his words came out in a snarl.

"I was the entertainment at the party tonight. They threw food at me before the evening devolved into one big orgy."

Bas rattled the bars. "Did anyone lay their hands on you?"

I had avoided that fate so far and would do everything in my power to continue avoiding it. "Aside from the guards carrying me to the bath, then the great hall and back, no. They didn't lay a hand on me. There were plenty of threats and promises of what awaits me. We have to get the hell out of here before that happens."

"No one will ever lay a hand on you. Can you access any of your power?"

I shook my head. "Not a drop of it. But Vodor can. He's been draining me ever since I got here. How long has it been anyway?"

Sebastian started pacing the length of his cell. "It's only been a day and a half. It took me too long to get away from my parents then make my way here without being stopped. I need to break us out of here before my grandmother's vision comes true."

"What do you mean? Was it her prophecy that everyone's been talking about?"

"No, she stopped sharing what she saw centuries ago. This was about my fate."

"You know you can't say that and not share more."

He shook his head and paused to throw me a look. "She told me I would die in the palace. She said my heart would lead me to my destiny, and that would end with my death. At least that was how she interpreted the dark vision of me in this cell."

"Why didn't you say something before? You should never have come back to fight with us."

"I wasn't about to let you fight Vodor without me. I didn't return to Eidothea for centuries because I was trying to avoid the fate my grandmother predicted for me."

"Maybe it's not valid anymore because Thelvienne didn't bring you back." There was no way I would allow him to die in that cell.

He snorted and narrowed his eyes. "I never would have come here for her. But I don't plan on dying down here. I have too much to live for."

"Oh." *Real eloquent, Fi. He's probably blown away by your gushing over his declaration.* He didn't have to tell me he loved me. That proved it more than words ever could. "You will make it out of here. I'll make sure of it." I braced myself on the bars as I tried for the thousandth time to find a way out of our current predicament. There was an answer. I just needed to find it.

# CHAPTER 19

"I'm not just a Fae. I'm also a witch." I embraced the truth of those words with every cell of my being. I hadn't ever distinguished one from the other before and wasn't certain I could do so now.

Putting every ounce of hope I had left in me into this wild thought working, I concentrated on removing the cuffs around my wrists. "*Intermissum.*" I held my breath for several seconds, waiting for my witchcraft to work. There was no way Vodor could block both sides of me. He was full-blooded Fae with no dual nature.

I could not allow Sebastian to die in this cell because of me. I refused to help his grandmother's vision come true. He didn't deserve this fate. He'd moved realms to avoid this very thing. Rage became a living thing in my chest. Evil could not continue to win.

My body heated as my anger increased until I thought I was going to spontaneously combust. My skin felt tight and brittle with the temperature rise. Right when I thought I would break apart, energy exploded from me in crackling light.

It illuminated the entire cavern and allowed me to see into the cracks and crevices. The Fae version of rats were swarming the dress I had discarded. The bottles that had broken on the shelves earlier had some kind of liquid in them because where it had spilled onto the floor, no plants were growing.

My cuffs popped open then dropped to the floor in a loud clatter. I rolled my wrists and winced when I got a good look at the tattered and bruised skin. A loud screeching sound filled the cavern, making my heart do a high jump in my chest.

The thick crust covering my river was gone, leaving me free access to both sides of my nature. The empty feeling was gone, and I was me again. It was simple for me to see through the spell of despair cast on the dungeon.

I lifted my hand to blow the door off the cell and barely stopped myself from casting it when Bas appeared and wrapped his hands around the metal. I was distracted by the way his muscles bulged. He was simply gorgeous. And strong as hell.

He pulled the door from its track and tossed it aside. I ran for him at the exact moment he came at me. I was in his arms and claiming his mouth in a hard, hungry kiss a second later.

I melted into him when his arms wound around me. I was no longer afraid. Hadn't been since I freed myself of the cuffs. The feeling of safety multiplied in his embrace. I ran my hands over his chest and around his neck as he deepened the kiss.

I wanted to lose myself in him and forget about everything else. He made it nearly impossible to stop from taking things further. Before we'd slept together, it had been too many years since I'd had sex. Tim had been sick for a couple years before he passed away over five years ago.

Now that he'd woken the beast, she was insatiable. I

wanted more from him. For several blissful seconds, I pushed reality aside and enjoyed the way his tongue danced with mine. I'd never been hornier just from kissing someone. Sebastian knew precisely how to prod my arousal into the stratosphere.

The earth started shaking around us, echoing what was going on in my *lady place*. I moaned into his mouth before breaking away when dirt and rocks fell onto our heads. "Crap. The earth really is trembling. I thought it was just me and what you do to my body."

Bas chuckled and pressed another quick kiss to my lips. "That's the cavalry arriving to help overthrow Vodor. Time to go, Butterfly."

I called up the elements, letting them fill me. Fire was at the fore, making me want to burn the place to the ground. As tempting as the idea was, I refused to jeopardize the palace. The successor would need the icon to help his transition to power.

Twining my fingers with Bas's, I paused at the tunnel entrance and lifted my free hand. "*Satiata.*" It was easy to yank earth to the surface, allowing it to gather the element and transport it to the dungeon.

We continued on as dirt started filling the space. Not wanting my handiwork to be undone, I flicked a hand over my shoulder. "*Induresco.*" Solidifying the enchantment made it that much harder for any Fae to remove the soil and open the dungeons. If the image of rebar reinforced cement I held in my mind had any say, it would be impossible.

With that taken care of, I took off in a run. My hair was matted to my head like a food-crusted helmet, and I stunk, but I had my battle gear, and my magic was back in full force. Adrenalin dumped into my bloodstream, boosting my energy. I was still running low from lack of food and sleep.

"How did you manage to free both of us from the restraints anyway?"

My feet slowed to a stop, and I glanced back at him. We were at the door to the house. "I thought you managed to get yours off. I realized Vodor couldn't block my witchcraft, so I used that to remove the cuffs and poured all the energy I could to make that happen."

"You're brilliant." Bas passed me and held the door open with a smile.

I smiled back at him and hurried into the lower sections of the palace. The passages were empty this far down, but I could hear screaming and fighting above us. I retraced my steps to the great hall, thinking Vodor was still there.

Servants were running with their arms full as we passed. I hoped they got away without being hurt. I didn't hold it against them for working for Vodor. Everyone had to do what they needed to survive.

The double doors were thrown open, noise from within spilled out into the hall. Surprisingly, I heard the distinct sound of metal on metal. They weren't only fighting with magic. Made sense given what my Grams told me about many factors impacting the stability of enchantments. Plus, I found it difficult to concentrate while fighting, which was why I ended up killing the Queen and absorbing her powers rather than Incapacitating her.

I had fireballs in my palms when I rushed into the room. The flowers that had adorned the tables were now wilted. There were bodies and scorch marks and overturned tables. I saw a group of women that had taunted me while they were throwing food at me.

I tossed one of the fireballs at them, then focused on the soldiers fighting what I surmised were members of the rebellion. They all wore battle gear similar to what I had on. My second fireball hit a soldier in the back of the head, making it pop like a grape.

Blood, brain, and bone rained down on Aislinn. "Ais! I was so worried." My fist was in motion as I spoke and slammed into the side of a guard's head. At least it was easy to tell the bad Fae apart. They wore the King's red uniform.

The other men and women who had participated in my humiliation wore fancy clothes and were easy to spot. I struggled with attacking them or not. At the moment, they weren't doing anything to indicate which side they were on. It seemed they were closer to sheep than anything with an autonomous brain.

"We have been going crazy wondering what Vodor was doing to you. Violet and I knew you were alive, but Bas didn't. Have you seen him? He came to find you?" I stopped next to Aislinn and kicked her opponent while she punched him. He threw jets of water at us.

"Ow. That freakin hurt," I cried out when what felt more like a razor sliced through my side. My top had lifted, allowing the spell to cut through my skin. "Sebastian was captured, but we both managed to escape. Where's Violet?"

"Somewhere in this mess." Aislinn dove forward to avoid being hit in the back of her skull. The dive morphed into a smooth summersault.

I tried to scan the room but couldn't see through the dozens of soldiers. One of them spun his knives in his hands as he stalked toward me. I had to shift my gaze all around, so I missed when he cast a spell. I felt the energy zing through the room a split second before hurricane-force winds sent me flying through the air.

The moment the wind connected with my sternum, it knocked the breath from me. My mouth was moving and forming a cushion, so I didn't break my face again. It was just starting to feel like it might heal.

I fell into a soft cloud and rolled to my feet, snatching a sword that was on the floor. It was heavy and awkward. I managed to lift it, but I couldn't put much force behind the blow when I swung it at the soldier. Thankfully, my awkward lurch lodged it right into the base of his neck, where it met his shoulder.

I left the weapon stuck in his body and turned away from the spurting blood, then scanned the room. I was off to the side and out of the middle now. I dropped below an overturned table and used it as a shield. At the same time, I watched a group of women stalking toward Violet. She was fighting for her life.

I had no idea what the women had planned, but the knives they were carrying didn't bode well. Wanting to make them pay but not start a fire that would only make matters worse, I called up lightning. When my hands crackled with bolts of blue light, I threw it toward the women.

Enough bolts left my hands that each of the three women was hit with at least one, if not more. There was a sizzle in the air followed by the smell of burned flesh, and they dropped to the floor, twitching.

"You aren't going to win, Teague," one of the party-goers called out from somewhere to the side. "You should have given her up sooner. Maybe you and your family would be spared."

I froze mid-crouch as I was standing up. Had Teague given me up? The betrayal tasted bitter on my tongue. It shouldn't surprise me, but it did. I couldn't see where Teague was until he spoke. "I told you a hundred times I will never side with you. You got lucky when you stumbled across her. And now we're here to make sure you don't get away with hurting anyone anymore."

My heart slowed, and I let out the breath I had been holding. I shouldn't have doubted him, but it was highly suspicious, and he didn't like me at all. I stood up without bothering to find him and raced toward Violet.

A soldier caught my attention halfway to my friend. She was moving stiffly, but she was wielding her magic with precision. I stood still with my focus on Violet instead of turning toward the guard coming for me. I needed him to get closer. While I stood there, I noticed something off about Violet's demeanor. It might be nothing more than the battle we were engaged in, but it might be more.

I didn't have time to consider that anymore. The soldier was a couple feet away, so I spun toward him and threw a broken glass at his face. It distracted him enough for me to kick him in the chest. Hands wrapped around my ankle before I lowered it back to the floor.

Darnell sneered at me and twisted the leg harshly. There was a pop followed immediately by pain in my right hip. I screamed and pulled him toward me. Dark energy pulsed throughout the castle, making me sick to my stomach. It stopped everyone, including the soldiers.

Kelvhan punched Darnell, and Darnell let go of my leg. Sebastian ran to my side a second later while the rest of the room came out of a stupor.

Bas grabbed my arm and turned to the door. "The King is up to something."

"And it's not good. We need to find him now and end this once and for all." I limped and fought nausea with every step. We were close to the exit and left the others to fight the soldiers as we left the great hall.

Out in the hallway, I grabbed his arm. "I need a second. My hip is dislocated. I'm not sure how long I will last like this. I need to pop it back in." The blood was being cut off to the limb, and the longer I waited, the more danger I was in. It would be challenging to maneuver into place without consistent pressure on my leg.

Sebastian regarded me with a furrowed brow. "How can I help?"

I grimaced then laid on the floor with Bas watching me with one brow raised. "Get your mind out of the gutter. I need you to shove it back into place. It'll be faster than me trying on my own. All you need to do is hold my leg at the knee and push it forward."

"Alright." His big, warm hands landed on my leg, he shifted it, and I nodded my head. Apparently, I didn't need to guide him anymore because when it was lined up from what I could tell, he shoved hard.

"Ahhh!" I swear my scream echoed throughout the hallway and into the great hall. The soul-searing pain diminished a second later.

I lifted my hand toward him. He clasped my hand and helped me to my feet. "Where do you think Vodor is?"

Sebastian shook his head. "First, are you alright?"

"I'll be fine. And I won't lose my leg now. But we have to stop him. Can you feel the power building?"

"I felt the initial wave, but I can't feel anything now. I think he's draining his soldiers. They aren't fighting as hard anymore." Bas's gaze was focused on the door to the hall.

"How can you...never mind that. Doesn't matter. We need to go this way." I headed toward the stairs on our left and climbed. We had to dodge into doorways when patrols passed at one end of the hall or the other.

It was easy to locate where Vodor was doing his spell in the heart of the palace. I had no idea what floor we were on, but the room Vodor was in was the only thing on that floor.

Before I could stop him, Sebastian had opened the door. He never made it into the room. His body went flying through the air. He hit the wall and fell to the floor in a heap, leaving a body-sized dent in the plaster.

I had to bite my tongue until it bled to keep from screaming. I didn't want to let Vodor know I was there. I scanned Sebastian for any sign he was alive. "Bas," I whispered, then knelt down and felt for a pulse. It was slow, but there.

Reassured by that, I crawled to the side of the door then poked my head around to see what was going on. Vodor was surrounded by dark energy and was looking out the window at the moment.

I ducked back behind the wall and called all of my elements to me. My river was now a tsunami inside my chest. It made my body sing, and my vision sharpen.

There were potions and a massive collection of energy in a large dark blue crystal in the far corner. It was obviously vital to whatever he was doing. I shot to my feet and raced inside the room. I had my elements poised and ready to eliminate the crystal.

A dark chuckle left Vodor's throat as he laid eyes on me. I released my elements and directed it to the corner. He lifted a hand and intercepted it. Lightning flashed outside the window, lighting up the dark clouds in the sky.

A curse left me when my elements tore through the glass and shattered it. Energy cut through my arm, nearly severing it. I called forth my fire and hoped it would cauterize the bleeding.

I should have been terrified, but I wasn't. I used that tsunami and directed it toward my wound while jumping to the side at the same time. I had more momentum than I realized and ended up sliding into the crystal. I kicked it to the broken window and wanted to shout when it cracked down the center.

I was on my butt, scooting backward with one arm hanging limply at my side. Vodor stalked toward me, and I noticed one of his hands was turning black. The dark energy was swirling faster and faster. I threw lightning at Vodor and kept the hits coming.

He tossed a fireball at me that hit my arm. It was bleeding, but not profusely, and his fire, while it hurt like a mother, helped seal the vessels and keep me from bleeding out. I twisted my hand and tossed a bolt of lightning at the massive blue crystal that was now black.

The crystal exploded like a firework. The force was so great it laid me out. My good arm went to my head to protect my face and eyes. Vodor screamed, and I tried to get up and go to him, but I couldn't move.

Turns out I didn't need to. A loud roar shook the walls. Sebastian. I lowered my arm and watched as Bas charged Vodor and grabbed hold of the sides of his head. I narrowed my lightning and aimed for Vodor's throat at the same time Bas twisted.

Bile rose in the back of my throat when Vodor's head left his shoulders. The King's body fell to the floor, and Bas was left holding his head. A blast of energy exploded out of the King's body.

The walls were blown out with the force, and so were the windows. The entire structure shook at the same time the stream traveled into my chest, stealing my breath. It filled me to the point I thought I was going to burst.

My heart raced so fast, it hurt. My good arm fell to the floor, and my vision darkened around the edges. Dust floated through the air, but the dark energy was gone entirely. I turned my head, trying to get a look at my injured arm. I didn't want to lose the limb.

My eyes landed on Sebastian, who tossed Vodor's withering head aside and dropped to his knees next to me. "I've got you, Fiona."

"Nnnn." I gave up trying to tell him to save my arm when the darkness won, and I lost consciousness.

# CHAPTER 20

I rolled to my side and groaned when pain ricocheted throughout my body. Everything hurt. Even my hair, but my arm hurt the worst, followed by my hip. I would have thought I slept funny, but they were on opposite sides of the body. Sometimes getting old sucked.

The second the thought raced through my mind, it was followed by the events that had just happened. I must have passed out after Sebastian, and I killed Vodor. I tried to sit up, but a large hand stopped me.

"It's okay, Butterfly. You're safe, and your arm is being stitched up." Bas's warm voice was laced with concern but soothing all the same.

I unsuccessfully tried to open my eyes. I didn't bother trying to wipe them clear. As if reading my mind, Sebastian placed a wet cloth over them and rubbed gently. Moving wasn't possible right then, so I let him care for me while trying to listen for danger. I didn't think he would be so calm if we still faced an entire army of enemies, but I had to be sure.

By the time the cloth was moved, I could blink and was

surprised to see Violet hovering over me with the rag in her hand. She'd been the one cleaning my eyes, not Sebastian. "Violet." It was so good to see her. I had been worried about her and Aislinn while fighting Vodor.

The sun was bright behind her head and burned my eyes. "I'm here. We're okay. Most of the soldiers stopped fighting as soon as you killed Vodor. Those that didn't were easy to handle." Violet's smile didn't reach her eyes. The fine lines around her eyes and mouth were more profound, and I could see the flaming bird still on her chest through a tear in her top.

"How long was I out?" My heartbeat rapidly a dozen times before slowing to its normal rhythm.

I tried to sit up, and Sebastian's gorgeous face filled my line of sight. "Relax. He's almost done. And you've only been out for a couple hours."

My head turned to the side. At first, I saw grass and flowers all around us and people sitting and lying on said grass. Then my gaze landed on a Fae pointing to my shoulder with his finger. There was a sting, and I saw blue energy slide through the sides of my wound and pull it together, exactly like he was using monocryl to stitch the deep laceration up.

"We're twins now," Violet teased. "We have matching injuries. Although you managed to heal mine without leaving much of a scar."

The healer paused and sniffed haughtily. "A scar is unavoidable with an injury like this."

Violet pulled the torn top of her battle gear aside and pointed to her shoulder. "Fiona didn't leave one on me." She was right. There wasn't even a thin red line. That boggled my mind more than anything else in my new magical life had. I'd seen too many wounds throughout my career and knew she should have had a thick raised scar along with function deficits.

"Did everyone make it?" Changing the subject seemed prudent. I didn't need this to devolve into an argument. Besides, I had to know that Aislinn and my other friends were alright.

"Argies is in bad shape, and many of the rebellion were killed, but the Backside of Forty are back together again." I gasped when I heard Aislinn's voice behind Violet.

It wasn't until Violet shifted that I caught sight of Aislinn kneeling next to Argies. I couldn't see much of him, but it was clear he was in bad shape given the three healers working on him.

"What happens for Eidothea now?" I cared about how they would move forward, but I had no desire to stay and help them work it out. I needed to return home and see Grams. I had to know she was still with me.

Violet's gaze shifted around whatever lawn we were camped out on. I imagined it was probably the courtyard of the palace. I could smell the remnants of a fire nearby. Had to be the damage that was done to the building.

Sebastian brushed the hair from my face. "They've already started talking about selecting a new King. Usually, there is a transfer of power from one ruler to the next, but that never happened with Vodor, so no one is entirely sure what to do now."

There was something he wasn't telling me. "Is there something I have to do to give back…" Bas pressed a finger to my mouth, cutting off the rest of my reply.

"You've done enough for the realm. It's time for you to rest and recover." He didn't want me to say anything else about what happened when Vodor died. I listened to him because I felt that knowing I absorbed the power from both would place a target on my back.

Violet bobbed her head. "Bas is right. Finarr assured me there are ceremonies to retrieve the previous King and

Queen's power and imbue the next. Many believe Vodor never possessed the core of the throne. It connects the rulers to every creature in the realm. They never would have been able to their power if they possessed it."

"All done. It will take several days for the flesh to completely knit back together, so take it easy." The healer brushed his hands off and climbed to his feet.

Sebastian helped me sit up then, and I smiled at the petite Fae. I hadn't realized how short he was when he had been kneeling next to me. "Thank you for helping me."

He inclined his head then moved on. I scanned the area, noting we were behind the palace, and the lawn was covered in dozens of injured Fae. Soldiers and rebellion members were working together. The thing that caught my attention was the fact that the oppressive atmosphere was gone.

"I'm ready to go home," I announced.

Violet brushed her arm over her forehead. "More than ready. I need to get back before the twins burn my house down."

Aislinn's smile disappeared as she chewed on her bottom lip. "I, uh, yeah. Going home would be good." Her gaze shifted from us down to Argies.

"You can stay here until he heals." I didn't want to return without her, but I wouldn't deny her the possibility of happiness.

She shook her head from side to side. "No. I need to get home and make sure I still have a job. Bills don't pay themselves, you know?"

"No, they certainly don't." I turned to face Sebastian. "Are you coming back with us? I know I haven't told you what I've been thinking or feeling. What I can say is that I can't imagine my life without you in it, and I don't want to."

He leaned forward and pressed an all too brief kiss to my lips. "I'm glad you finally said that. I had planned on returning and doing whatever it took to convince you that we belong together. I want you to be my mate."

I thought married life was behind me forever, and yet this somehow didn't surprise me. "What exactly does that mean? Is mating like marriage?"

Bas shook his head. "It's very different—Fae mate for life. Once we choose who we want, there is never anyone else for us. We live a long time, so we're talking centuries."

"I'm human. I won't live for centuries." I liked the idea of him only having eyes for me.

"You aren't actually human. From what Isidora shared with me, you can choose to age like normal, or you can embrace your magic and let it extend your life. But that's something we can deal with later. Just agree to be mine." His smile melted my mind into a puddle, and all I could think about was how much I wanted him.

No, wasn't even an option. "Since you asked so nicely, yes. First, let's get home."

I never imagined myself embroiled in a magical war, yet here I was, killing it. I was no longer the ignorant neophyte. I knew just enough to be dangerous. I wasn't dumb enough to think life would be a walk in the park from now on. There was still a murderer traipsing around Cottlehill Wilds, so we still had crap to deal with, but I wasn't alone in this. I had my best friends and Sebastian. The Backside of Forty was ready to handle any chaos life tossed our way.

WE SAID goodbye to Finarr and the others. I was worried about Aislinn, who looked reluctant to leave Argies behind. I heard her sneak off several nights to be with the guy but kept that to myself. We needed all the happiness we could get.

Having this issue behind us was an enormous relief, but it

was just one of the crises we'd faced. Life had been one adrenaline-fueled moment after another ever since Grams died and I moved to Pymm's Pondside.

I wondered if Violet was getting flak from her original coven. I pondered for the thousandth time what her responsibilities were to them. There were no doubt, duties that she'd been shirking to help me and the war in Eidothea. I'd bet that was what had her occupied.

I clasped hands with Sebastian and opened the portal. This time the oval shimmered to life in the middle of the stone archway I had hauled around the realm with me. It wavered, and a second later, I saw the bones that formed the tether on our side.

"You know where to reach us if you need anything," Sebastian told his parents and Finarr. I was surprised they'd decided to see us off. They had warmed to me but didn't look happy that Bas wanted to mate me.

Violet and Aislinn said their goodbyes and crossed through. Sebastian and I were next. I was familiar with crossing now that I wasn't put off when darkness encompassed me between one step and the next. As expected, my hair whipped around my head in the wind created in the portal.

My arm ached as we traveled through the dark tunnel. I couldn't wait to take a hot shower and put some sweats on. It had been a long ass day of cleaning and searching for survivors in the palace, and I had been covered in filth before it even began.

I decided not to wait to bathe there. I just wanted to return to Grams. Light flashed around me, making black spots dance in my vision, and then I was being squeezed through a tight space. The compression around me disappeared, and I took the next step into the now recreated crypt.

When and how did Grams rebuild the building that had

been destroyed? I rushed forward and wrapped my arms around the diminutive woman I had been terrified would be gone when I returned.

"You're alive! I was so worried you wouldn't be here when we got back."

Grams patted my back and pushed me away. "I'm as surprised as you are. Camille seems to think I'll be around until you get the hang of your powers."

"That would be fantastic. Although I never want to let you go. Can't you, you know, just choose not to age?" Her shocked look made me chuckle. "Yeah, Bas told me about that one, although I don't know much more than that really."

I noticed there was no door on the mausoleum as we exited into the family cemetery. "I thought you were going to wait for me to rebuild this."

Grams narrowed her eyes. "I got bored. Do you have any idea how hard it is to sit in that house and not be able to leave?"

"Were you stuck here?" My mind was immediately working through solutions. I didn't want her to be relegated to Pymm's Pondside.

"I couldn't exactly go to the store or Mug Shots for a sandwich. I'm supposed to be dead."

"Oh. That's right. So how have things been around here while we were gone? And where did Violet and Aislinn go?"

"They went to shower and get changed. I imagine you'll want to clean up, as well." Her nose wrinkled as she looked at me.

The hand I lifted to my hair almost got stuck in the gunk. "I'd better clean this off before it sinks deeper into my skin, and I carry around the stink permanently. I won't belong."

Grams waved me away when we entered the house, and I darted upstairs, leaving Bas to catch up with her. I flipped the water on hot in my bathroom and shucked the battle gear as fast as possible. I had to go slowly because the pain in my shoulder flared high enough to steal my breath.

I avoided the mirror. There were some things a girl didn't need to see, and this was one of them. Once under the flow, I scrubbed my hair one-handed and used a generous amount of shampoo and conditioner.

It felt so good to wash away the food, blood and God only knew what else. It took me scrubbing my scalp three times for the water to run clear. Once done, I reluctantly shut the water off and discovered Sebastian waiting with a towel in hand.

My initial reaction was to hide my body. No one wanted to see the stretch marks, saggy boobs, and wrinkles. Except he looked at me with heat in his eyes, telling me he liked what he saw.

"While I would love to explore that look in your eyes further, the others are waiting downstairs. Camille just arrived with news she wanted to wait to share with all of us."

"Then you better go." I took the towel from him and wrapped it around my torso. Bas watched as I dried off quickly then stepped into my underwear and sweats. He helped with the t-shirt, and I grabbed my socks and headed for the door with them in hand.

"You look much better," Aislinn called out when we entered the family room.

Grams had prepared tea and snacks, and they were on the coffee table, which I sat down in front of. "I feel much better. Good to see you, Camille. I hear you have some news for us."

Camille inclined her head and set her teacup on the table next to the recliner she was sitting in. "I'm glad you guys are back. Things here have gotten worse. Whoever is killing paras has stepped up their game. There have been three deaths since you left a few days ago. The latest was Sterling. I believe he was your neighbor, Aislinn."

I rubbed my temples. "I had really hoped we'd have a few days to rest. I can't do much with my arm in this condition."

Grams' sharp eyes shifted to me. "What do you mean? What condition is your arm in?"

I proceeded to tell them what had happened after we crossed to Eidothea, leaving out how I had absorbed Vodor's power. That was something I would share with Grams when we were alone, but not before.

"I might be able to help with that." Grams moved to sit next to me and laid her hands on my injured shoulder. "We have to do something to stop whoever is stalking our kind."

Heat traveled from her hand and sunk into me, making my arm tingle. "We will find whoever is responsible tomorrow. None of us are up to playing detective again so soon."

While the others answered questions about what Eidothea was like and more details about what was going to happen now, I poured some tea and grabbed a scone. I felt like I hadn't eaten in too damn long.

By the time I had inhaled three cinnamon chip scones, my stomach had settled, and I was leaning against Bas as we talked. Camille had specific thoughts about one of the witch elders being responsible for the deaths. I only heard half of what she said. I was busy enjoying the shift in my new magical life.

I had no idea what was ahead for us, but I had Aislinn, Violet, and Sebastian there to support me every step of the way. Together there wasn't anything we couldn't handle.

* * *

*Violet*

I pulled into the driveway, glad to see the lights on inside. My heart had stopped when Camille told us about the deaths. She was mad at me for being MIA when the coven needed me. The elders had united witches decades before I was even born, and it had been our duty to ensure it functioned properly.

Being part of a prominent coven was far more complicated than being part of the Backside of Forty. We had each other's backs and did what needed to be done. There were no political disputes or duties to perform to ensure the elders had the spells and potions they required to ensure mundies didn't happen upon Cottlehill Wilds.

Putting the car in park, I turned off the ignition and got out. The breath I had been holding rushed out of me when Ben opened the front door. "Hey, mom. You gonna sit there all night? I need you to talk some sense into your daughter."

I released the breath I had been holding. Ever since Camille mentioned she suspected Adam was responsible had me on edge. I never would have imagined a fellow witch could be accountable for such atrocities. And if Adam was the one doing it, I worried he might be inclined to make me pay for rejecting him over a decade ago when I went through my divorce.

After Ben and Bailey had been kidnapped, I kept having nightmares about their gruesome deaths or being forced to watch them be tortured. I hardly slept. And then something in me shifted when we were in the Fae realm.

It happened shortly after I almost lost my arm. Fire built in my chest and spread out, burning me from the inside out. When the flames finally died, I was no longer me. My energy and magic felt different enough that I had yet to try and cast a spell. I would need to soon to determine if it was all in my head or not.

And then there was the bird on fire on my chest. I knew it meant something, but I had no idea. I would need to check my family's grimoire for answers. But first, I had to deal with the latest fight between my kids.

The fact that they were arguing again was music to my ears. They hadn't been after we rescued them and coupled with the changes I was going through, I was certain nothing in my life would ever be the same again. And I wasn't sure that was a good thing.

"What's going on now? What are you arguing about this time?" I headed up the walk and was on the second step leading up to the porch when Bailey stuck her head out beside her brother's.

"He wants to go to the states and live with Fiona's kids while we go to college at UNC." Bailey glared at Ben with her arms crossed over her chest.

My heart skipped several beats, and my eyes flared. I lowered my head and continued walking until we were all in the house. I wasn't ready for them to leave at all. They weren't full witches like I was, so we didn't know if they would take after their father, who was a merman, or me.

"I didn't realize that was one of your choices. Have you spoken with Emmie about the possibility of staying there?"

Ben's cheeks heated, and he lowered his head. "I talk to her all the time, and she said now that they had their parent's house, there was plenty of room for us."

"But I don't want to leave England. Dad doesn't want us to go either." My eyes swung to Bailey when she mentioned their father.

"When did you talk to him?" If Trent had told her that he would fight any move with everything he had. He could swim across oceans easily to visit the kids, but he had duties to the clan near England. It was one of the reasons he left us over a decade ago.

"He came to see us a couple days ago," Ben replied.

I set my purse down and headed for the sofa. "Did you tell him where I was?"

Both the twins shook their heads. "He didn't ask, so we

didn't tell him." I could kiss Bailey. They both were protective of me, but she would have sooner eaten dirt than tell him something he could use to hurt me.

We got along for the most part unless something happened. He automatically blamed me no matter what. I was sick of everything being my fault which was why we never told him about the kidnapping.

"This is a conversation we need to have with him before any decisions are reached. For now, why don't you catch me up on what's been going on around here."

Ben took the chair, and Bailey sat next to me. They both launched into a discussion about how the bonfire at the cliffs had been canceled the night before, and everyone was pissed. I listened to them talk and thought about how quiet and lonely the house would be without them.

Perhaps it was time for me to start a new life like Fiona had. I had no plans to move to another country like she did. And I already knew about my magic and how to use it. Or did I?

As a matter of fact, no, I had no idea what I was capable of now. My magic was utterly foreign to me, and I had a lot to learn. Looked like I was getting my own new beginning. If I was lucky, mine would come with a broody, sexy Fae like Fiona's had.

# EXCERPT FROM MAGICAL MAKEOVER BOOK #1 MYSTICAL MIDLIFE IN MAINE

"What do you mean that was an irritated ghost?" I gaped at my patient as she lay on her hospital bed and shrugged her shoulders. Surreptitiously, I checked to make sure I hadn't peed myself a little. Ever since I had my daughter, my bladder control went out the window with sleep.

How was this my life now? I'd gone from being Charge Nurse at a respected hospital in the triangle in North Carolina, married to one of the country's best cardiothoracic surgeons to divorced and living back home with my mother and grandmother.

Hattie Silva, my patient and current employer stared at me with a furrowed brow. She was a ninety-year-old woman suffering from cancer of the intestines and required full-time care. After being fired from the hospital, my ex-husband ran me out of North Carolina and had managed to ruin my reputation, leaving me no options for work outside of in-home nursing with a hospice organization.

"I mean precisely what I said. Evanora isn't happy about

you ignoring her. She's trying to get your attention. I struggle to hear her most days. I'm at the end of my life and running out of time." Hattie looked frail when she spoke like that.

She was older and suffering far more than was pleasant. It was difficult to watch her in so much pain, but when she talked like this it was easy to forget all of that and simply see her as crazy. I thought her doctors needed to dementia to her diagnoses.

I reached up and grabbed the necklace Fiona had sent to me a few weeks ago. My best friend had moved to England after her grandmother had died and started a new life without me. At first, I kept busy with the kids and Miles, but when my ex informed me that he was leaving me for another woman and proceeded to tear my life apart like a wrecking ball, I missed Fiona more than ever.

We met in college and hit it off right away. We'd been in each other's weddings, got jobs at the same hospitals and did everything together. I was there when her twins were born because her husband Tim had gotten stuck in traffic. And she was there for me for both of mine. Miles had elected to continue surgeries both times saying it was too complicated for him to hand off.

My heart skipped a beat when the bluish image of a woman wearing a bonnet with a tall brim and a floor length dress that was cinched around the waist with big, poofy sleeves appeared in the spot where the remote control had fallen. Startled, I dropped the necklace and reached my hand toward the ghost. The image disappeared and I shivered with the chill in the air.

*Great, now she was infecting me with her crazy.* Ignoring what I thought I saw, I set the glass of water on the tray beside the bed and raised the head of her bed more. "There's no such thing as ghosts. Let's get you some lunch. I made some chicken soup today."

Hattie was so thin I could see her bones under her flesh. She felt very breakable when I shifted her body's position. She started coughing when she slumped forward to make it easier for me to arrange her support. As gently as possible, I laid her on the pillows and held the cup in front of her mouth then adjusted the oxygen flowing through her nasal cannulas.

After several seconds, she took a sip then sighed. "How is it you have an item of Power, but you are ignorant as the day is long?"

This was a familiar argument. She would say something about me having some powerful object and being ignorant of everything important around me. "I like you too, Hattie. You ready for lunch?" At her nod, I left to get the food. The house was massive and most of the time I didn't notice the echo throughout the place, but I was jumpy after that conversation about spirits.

Rumors from my childhood popped into my head. Maybe they had been right after all. It would make sense for her to believe in ghosts if she really was a powerful witch. Although, I could see only brief glimpses of the power she must have once held. Whether or not that was true didn't matter.

She was ill and susceptible to being taken advantage of. I hadn't been hired to consider anything other than her health, but I would never sit by and allow someone to take her for a ride. Hattie was richer than God and had numerous companies to her name. All of which poachers were dying to get their hands on. *Not on my watch.*

Hurrying to the kitchen, I turned off the pot that had been simmering on low for the past half hour since I finished putting it together. I grabbed two bowls and paused when my gaze caught sight of the water beyond the window. The panoramic views of the Penobscot Bay were to die for and cost a fortune.

Hattie's house was called Nimaha. It reminded me of how Fiona had always called her grandmother's home Pymm's Pondside. Their generation must have named their houses or something. I'd heard several friends talking about names of their grandparents' homes. My generation had nothing as refined to lay claim to. We had crow's feet, liver spots and unwanted chin hair among other unpleasant signs of reaching middle age.

Wanting to shove aside thoughts that would only lead me to perseverate on how my life had gone to hell in a hand-basket at the most inopportune time in my life, I refocused on the coastline. There was nothing on the more than three hundred feet of shoreline. Hattie had a serene sanctuary here. The waves lapped lazily against the pebbled beach. It was so peaceful and remote. Nothing like the hustle and bustle of the big city hospital where I spent twenty years caring for patients. I watched for several seconds until my mind quieted and I was relaxed.

Turning away from the big window, I grabbed the rolls my grandmother had sent with me that morning and headed back through the five thousand square foot house. Thankfully I didn't have to clean all of the bedrooms and bathrooms, or care for the three acres and its outbuildings. The gardening alone had to be a beast to maintain, although I had yet to see a gardener come and tend to the multi-terraced back yard.

A hiss nearly made me drop the tray of soups I had been carrying. Shifting my hold on the tray, I scanned the area for the little heathen that I swore was trying to kill me. There she was.

"Don't scare me like that Tarja." The tabby cat stuck her nose in the air as if she could understand me and continued past me and up the stairs. She had the most beautiful coat I'd ever seen on a cat. Multi-colored with the oranges and yellows being vibrant and shiny.

The second bowl on the tray was to feed Tarja. I wasn't used to treating a cat like a person, but she ate the same food I fed Hattie. I swear Hattie invented the term crazy cat lady. Tarja was her Princess and the only thing Hattie was forceful about during the job interview. I should have known Hattie wasn't entirely together when she told me Tarja was to be fed meals with her and her litter box needed to be cleaned several times a day.

I could deal with Hattie's eccentricities and bed pan and dressing changes without any problems. It was cleaning animal feces from a box that made me gag. Yes, I was aware how little sense that made. But c'mon it was a container filled with excrement that had been sitting for hours.

Shrugging off that unpleasant thought, I continued climbing the stairs and stopped short when I saw a large creature through the port hole window on one of the landings. It was dark green and almost as tall as the closest tree. And it looked the dragons Hollywood depicted in countless movies. Only I didn't see any wings on this one.

What the heck was that? I swear something new popped up every day in this place. My heart raced and I was nearly hyperventilating as I tried to figure out what the large beast was. My breaths fogged the glass, making me use the sleeve of my top to clear the glass. When I looked back out there was nothing there.

When another scan didn't come up with the dragon, I continued up the stairs and hurried into Hattie's room where I deposited the tray and rushed to the window. Her room faced the side of the house where I'd seen the dragon. I hoped I would catch sight of it. Something that big wouldn't be able to disappear into the forest surrounding her without leaving a trail.

"What are you in a tither about now?" Hattie snapped at me like this more often than not. It was how someone talked to their child when they'd had enough of their odd behaviors.

I turned to my patient and pushed the table with the tray of food over to the bed. "I thought I saw a dragon in your backyard. I'm losing my mind just as much as you are it seems. Must be the stress of the divorce."

Hattie laughed, the sound like dry leaves rattling over a sidewalk. "You aren't seeing things, my dear. That was Tsekani. Oh, that soup smells delicious."

I was too tired to let my surprise show over her having named this imaginary dragon. *Are you sure it's not real? You saw if for yourself.* I was positive it was a bad sign that my mind was trying to rationalize my hallucinations.

I set the bowl I had brought for me down on the floor on the plate I had the rolls on. "Here's your lunch, Tarja."

The cat approached and sniffed the soup then started lapping it up. "She says the bay leaves were a good addition to the soup. That's not something I've ever added to mine."

My head snapped up to meet Hattie's smile. "What?"

"Seriously. Where did you get that necklace from? I'm beginning to sense you aren't magical at all." Everything in me froze with her words, including my heart for several seconds.

"My best friend, Fiona had made it for me as a symbol of my new beginning. Why are you saying it's magical? There's no such thing." Right? I wanted to believe I was open minded, but the past month of working for Hattie Silva and hearing her bizarre comments had me questioning that.

There was no way I could jump on board with her and believe in magic.

Although, I had to admit I was beginning to have my doubts. I'd seen enough in the past four weeks to really wonder. Problem was that I'm a scientist and relied on what I could prove and see. And while I had seen more than a fair share of oddities there was nothing I could hold onto or exam all that closely.

"You wouldn't believe me if I told you. Can you push the tray closer? I'd like to taste the soup Tarja can't shut up about." I shook my head and moved the tray over her bed and adjusted it, so she was able to reach her food easily.

I picked up a roll and tore off chunks while staring out the window. She had windows facing the forest and another on the wall above her head that overlooked the water. I was focused on the gentle waves and the pebbled beach when a dog raced across the area, kicking up rocks as he went.

My feet carried me closer and I watched as he bared his teeth. He wasn't like any dog I'd ever seen. He was big and dark grey in coloring. "Do you have wolves in this area?"

The clatter of a spoon filled the room. "Of course. Layla moved here first, but several others have taken refuge here over the years." I wasn't surprised to discover she named the wolves prowling in her woods. She had named her house after all. Wild wolves wouldn't have been my first choice of companions, but she had enough property to safely offer a place to as many wild animals as she wanted.

Dark coughing made me turn away from the window. I expected it to be Hattie, but it was Tarja. If she hocked up a hairball, I wasn't cleaning it. "When does your maid come to clean the house anyway? I've never met her."

Hattie cocked her head to the side and looked at me. "Mythia comes after you leave. She doesn't care to be around mundies. Why?"

*Mundies?* "I have no idea what that means, but I assure you I have done nothing to upset anyone. I haven't been here long enough to make any enemies. I was hoping to talk to her about how she gets rid of hard water around the shower faucet. I have never been able to get mine so clean."

I thought moving home would offer me a few perks. Like not having to clean bathrooms anymore, but I'd been wrong. There was no way I could take advantage of my mother like Miles had me for so many decades. Despite working long hours seven days a week I always pulled my weight around the house.

After the hurt of his announcement settled in, I immediately began dreaming about what my life would be like without him. In my naivete I had dreamed of continuing my position at the hospital and staying in the house and hiring someone to do the cleaning.

Reality was an entirely different beast. After being fired I had spent weeks of job hunting before realizing I had no choice but to move home. Miles's little tart worked in human resources at the hospital and made sure I wasn't appealing to anyone interested in hiring me. I could have filed a suit for violating my rights, but after Miles had managed to fast track our divorce and screw me out of what I deserved I didn't bother. He had friends in high places.

"Oh, I know you haven't. I did my research before hiring you. Speaking of, how did you piss off Tara so thoroughly? She had nothing good to say about you when I called. And Mythia won't share her secrets with me, so she won't share anything with you."

My head started pounding and I clenched my jaw then balled my hands into fists. Miles got his little girlfriend to sabotage my only shot at a job in this area, too? "Tara is the jailbait that slept with my husband and blacklisted me at all the hospitals in North Carolina. My ex-husband didn't want to be reminded of what a jerk he is or that his girlfriend isn't much older than our son."

Hattie laughed so hard she started coughing. Tarja jumped onto her lap and placed a paw on her chest. Their connection was more than obvious. The cat was always close and offering comfort when Hattie had bad moments. I shifted Hattie forward and rubbed circles on her back until she stopped coughing.

"I was right about that one it seems. When I saw the written record of your employment, it made no sense to me that you suddenly started making fatal mistakes after twenty years of pristine performance reviews. She did her best to convince me that you were stressed out and upset over your husband leaving you and could no longer be trusted with patients."

I gently set her against the pillows again and returned to the window. "I was upset that Miles left me like he did, but it never affected my ability to do my job. I can assure you I will not cause you harm in any way."

Hattie waved a hand dismissively. "Oh, I know that dear. What do you say we curse her with premature winkles? Or maybe make him impotent!"

That made me choke out a laugh as I turned away from the beach outside. "I would love nothing more, but that would make me like them, and I will never be so malicious. I believe that you reap what you sow. They will both get what's coming to them one day."

"You've got that right, dear. Fate gets her way, even if it takes years and several unexpected turns." I bobbed my head in agreement as I gathered the lunch dishes from her tray.

*****

I turned my Land Rover off and couldn't help but smile.

Keeping the nice SUV along with half of the house when it sold were the only concessions the Judge awarded me which was why I was forced to move back with my mom and grandmother.

I couldn't afford the house payments on the lake front house and no one would hire me. I couldn't buy a house on the money I would be given whether Miles sold or bought me out. We owed too much on the property.

Looking up at the house I had grown up in, I couldn't help but think about the differences between Hattie's house and the house I left back in North Carolina compared to this one.

My grandparents moved into this modest one-story Cape Cod style home almost seventy years ago. The yellow siding had been repainted half a dozen times and the windows were replaced with double-pained ones last summer. The kitchen had been updated fifteen years ago when my mom moved in with my grandmother but not much else had been done.

The wood floors were scuffed and scarred and the marks measuring my height were still in the doorway to the garage alongside my mother's. Unlocking the front door, I entered to the familiar smell of lemon polish and baking bread.

"I'm home," I called out as I set my keys in the dish on the table in the entrance. "Where is everyone?"

My mother poked her head out of the kitchen. "We're in here, just finishing up dinner. Did you eat with Ms. Silva?"

I headed down the hall and caught the door before it closed after my mother returned to the sink. "Hi, nana. How was your day?" I bent and kissed her cheek while she sat in a chair at the table. She was the same age as Hattie but in much better shape.

She patted my cheek and smiled up at me. "I made some rye bread for you to take to Hattie tomorrow and finished the book I was reading."

"And you got in a good nap," my mother interjected. "Anything new happen out at Nimaha today?"

Both enjoyed hearing about the events, saying the house had been haunted as long as they could remember. I shrugged my shoulders. "Hattie has given refuge to wild wolves living in the woods around her house and she has a dragon named Tsekani."

Grandma nodded her head. "She owns something like five acres, so she probably does think she is giving them a place to live. But a dragon? Is it dementia? Many of my friends have succumbed already."

My mother shut off the water and leaned against the counter drying her hands. "Good thing we have excellent genes, and you don't have to worry about that mom. You might want to start looking for another job soon, sweetie. Sounds like she's going downhill fast."

"Who's going downhill fast?" Nina asked as she entered the kitchen and approached me with her arms open.

"Ms. Silva," I replied for my mom and embraced my daughter. She looked a lot like me except her brown hair was longer than my short cut and she didn't have crow's feet around her brown eyes. I had always loved the fact that she looked so much like me. Until I was fairly certain that was the reason Tara didn't want Nina around anymore.

Nina released me and went to the fridge. "She's been cra-cra since the day you started there. You don't have to worry about finding another job." I could hear the panic in Nina's voice. She was by my side when I struggled to find a position and celebrated with me when Hattie hired me to take care of her.

"I am giving her gold start treatment to make sure she sticks around. Do you want me to make you a snack?"

Nina gave me a side smile and shook her head. "No, you

sit down and rest your feet. You work too hard. I'll grab you some rocky road."

I sat next to nana and held back the emotion choking me. I might not have the fancy house or the cushy job, but I had more love than Miles would ever know and that's all that mattered.

When my daughter asked my mom and grandmother what they wanted and proceeded to get them some vanilla ice cream along with a cookie, I realized Hattie didn't have this. She was all alone in the world and had no one to shower her with love and affection.

I made a silent vow to ignore the crazy and show her how much she was appreciated. She was cranky, and adored cats, but she was funny and made me laugh all the time. And there were times when she had these little nuggets of wisdom that were priceless. Like when she told me to stop complaining that my daughter was asking for a car of her own.

Hattie had just finished the cookies Nina had dropped off at the end of my first week on the job when I started complaining about her latest request. I would never forget the way Hattie had scowled at me as she said, *"Be grateful she doesn't want it to go joy riding. She wants to give you and your mother a break from taking her to and from practice, and a way to get to and from a job. Yeah, she told me how much she wanted to earn money to ease your burden. Most children her age are selfish critters with no care for anyone else, let alone how much their parents sacrifice to give them what they have."*

I blinked and shoved the memory aside when Nina kissed my cheek and placed the bowl in front of me. "Thank you, peanut. You're the best daughter ever born."

"Agreed." My mom and grandmother both spoke at the same time while enjoying their dessert. My midlife makeover wasn't what I had hoped it would be when I was twenty something, but I couldn't ask for more.

# EXCERPT FROM MY MAGICAL LIFE TO LIVE BOOK #4 MIDLIFE WITCHERY

"I am ready for life to settle without chaos and fighting evil." I loved having my best friend living full-time in Cottlehill Wilds for the past eight months, even though along with Fiona came trouble.

"You do realize you've jinxed us now. You're part of the magical world now. You can't go around inviting the bad guys to surface." I locked my bookstore and scanned the street. Ever since the first murder in our small town, I had a hard time walking home at night.

"We killed the evil King. There's no one left to attack us."

"Fiona Grace Shakleton. Watch your mouth. That's asking for trouble. Besides, we still have a murderer out there," Isidora, her grandmother, said in the background. It was still odd to hear her voice and see her. I was with Aislinn when we discovered her dead in the living room. None of us understood what Fiona did to bring her back to life or how long she would remain alive. All spells lost their power eventually unless you continued to feed it energy. You couldn't add to what you didn't understand.

Fiona sighed. "That's exactly what Violet just told me. Did Mae stop by today?"

I stuff my free hand into my purse and clutched my pepper spray. My magic had been acting up ever since I was injured in the battle in Eidothea, so I didn't want to rely on it in an emergency.

"She did. Apparently, Lance is stumped over the murder of that human months ago. It's no surprise that he is frustrated by the lack of leads. While the supernatural office of investigations is inundated with evidence. Gardoss reported that his office is analyzing as fast as they can. Mae said Gardoss told her they'd detected Dark, demonic magic."

"That's not surprising. Did any murders occur after we killed Vodor? Bas assured me his lackeys would have felt his demise and given up and gone into hiding."

"I didn't get a chance to ask her for more information. A customer came in, and she left. Did Isidora hear anything useful while we were gone?" The night closed around me like a cloak. Close and all-encompassing. It wasn't a pleasant sensation.

"She lost her connection to the dead when I resurrected her. The last thing she discovered was from Tunsall's sister when she crossed to the afterlife. Her murderer had grey skin and black horns on his head and red scales on his arms. Grams thought she was confused."

"A bilge changes their appearance and mimics other creatures when they kill, but they don't leave evidence behind. They wouldn't be the best assassins if they did. It doesn't make any sense." We were convinced the culprit was a *bilge,* one of the King's assassins. Now, it seemed unlikely. I was torn between hoping it was one and wanting it to be something else. Neither option was appealing.

"I never considered it as anything other than the *bilge.*

What Grams described sounds like a demon to me. Please tell me they don't exist."

"Unfortunately, they are real creatures. However, they don't cross through the veil that often," I said at the same time Grams responded in the background on Fiona's end of the call. "Of course, demons exist. And I would bet there is one stalking supernaturals in Cottlehill Wilds. Our town is a veritable buffet for a creature from the Underworld."

My heart picked up speed, making me dizzy for a split second. The skin where I had my new marking prickled and stung. During the fighting in the Fae realm, a Dark elf's spell sliced into my chest. When the skin healed, the image of a burning bird was left behind. Now it flared to life anytime my blood surged through my veins.

"That doesn't sound very good. Is there a system in place to deal with rogue demons on Earth? It sounds beyond Gardoss's ability to handle. He seems like a competent cop, but he isn't all-powerful or anything." Fiona wasn't wrong about that. Most in our law enforcement didn't have experience with anything demonic.

I looked into the shadows along the road as I walked past closed businesses. I had lived here all my life, yet it felt like a foreign town now. There was an energy in the night that I couldn't identify. At times, it seemed to be coming from me. And others, it was foreign magic outside of my body.

"Maybe it isn't a demon. We could be dealing with a sloppy bilge. The deaths have all looked as if various creatures were responsible. First, it seemed like a werewolf was the culprit. Then we found the dragon scale. Mae mentioned one with fang marks as if a vampire had drained her. That fits with our original theory. The Dark magic calls that into question. They don't mimic anything demonic." My head ached, and I wanted to forget all about these cases.

I wasn't a member of either the human or supernatural

law enforcement. This wasn't our responsibility. And yet, ever since Fiona moved to Cottlehill Wilds and became the new Guardian of the portal, I had joined her and Aislinn, and we'd fallen into that role. Gardoss wasn't the only one that didn't like us sticking our noses into each of his cases. I was getting pretty tired of it, as well.

Investigating cases excited me before I accompanied Fiona and Aislinn to Eidothea. Now, my body was changing, and my magic was on the fritz. I didn't have time to deal with this crap. An out-of-control witch was dangerous. Suppose Camille or Gardoss discovered I was having trouble. In that case, they'd want me incarcerated until they could be certain I wouldn't blow something up.

I pulled my hand out of my purse and tried to conjure a fireball on my palm. The flames sizzled and sputtered. Instead of going out, they shot into the air. I curled my fingers which should have smothered the fire. They were beyond my control and hit the bark of a tree in the distance.

"What was that? Are you alright?" Fiona's voice penetrated my mind and snapped me to attention.

"Yeah, sorry. I was just wondering if it could be someone trying to force us out into the open. Many paranormals have tried over the years, claiming we should be in positions of power over humans. Maybe it's someone trying to get Lance's attention."

"If that were the case, Lance would have been called to the scene of the deaths. The culprit would have made sure he became involved. Without him investigating, the existence of supernaturals wouldn't be revealed," Fiona countered.

"Good point. I feel like we're spinning in circles. The investigations are best left to Gardoss. We could all use some downtime. We had already saved one realm. This one will have to wait until we're all one hundred percent again."

Fiona chuckled. "What did you tell me months ago?

Something about evil not waiting for me to be at my best and to get off my ass and learn everything I could. You're my best friend, and I can't imagine facing this world without you. But if you need rest, you don't have to help with this. Aislinn, Bas, and I can handle it."

I considered that for one second. I wanted to tell her it wasn't a matter of getting sleep. My magic was on the fritz. The Fae realm fight did something to me that I couldn't figure out, and I wasn't working right at the moment.

"As if you could handle this without me. Someone has to be the voice of reason here. Plus, when the witch elders objected to bringing the SEA or Supernatural Enforcement Agency in on the deaths, they cited you as their reason. It was agreed that you are a force to be reckoned with, and for as long as anyone could remember, the Shakleton's and their Guardianship have extended to the town."

Isidora made a hmph sound. An image of her hovering next to Fiona as she listened to our conversation popped into my head. "Our family has always solved disputes and stepped in before disagreements got out of hand. We've earned the town's faith, but I don't think your elders want Fiona to handle the case out of the goodness of their hearts. It's about money. They don't have to pay her like they do Gardoss and SEA. They're cheap bastards."

A noise in the park up ahead froze my blood and my feet. I was on freaking edge and about to jump out of my skin. "There's something in the park," I whispered into the phone.

"What?" Fiona's whisper-yell echoed from my cell like a foghorn.

"Be quiet. I'm going to investigate. I sure wish I had driven to work tonight." About two years ago, when my husband left me, I started walking to work as a way of getting back in shape. Middle age had a way of creeping up on you and blindsiding you with random hair, body aches, hormone surges, and hot flashes.

As if I conjured the symptoms, heat barreled through my body, starting in my feet and heading for my scalp. Sweat dotted my skin in its wake. I resembled one of those hot dogs that roll around on a heater all day waiting for some unsuspecting victim to buy it.

I was breathing so hard I swore it was shining a light on my crouched position at the edge of the pavement. Walking toward the park while staying hunched down was slow going. The park was suddenly a mile away.

My thighs were burning like the pits of Hell by the time I reached the break in the hedges. I was steps away from the path into the park. Moving forward went against my desire to not get involved in the investigations. I've never waffled over decisions like this before.

On the one hand, I wanted to stand up and run in the other direction. While on the other I was ready to march into the park and stop whatever was happening. The malicious intent thickening the air and choking me told me whatever was happening wasn't a sexy rendezvous between lovers.

I placed my hand over my chest and poked my head around the bushes. At first, I didn't see anything. It was as I turned to vanish behind the shrub that I caught one glowing red eye. I sucked in a breath and ducked behind the plant to hide my presence.

It was definitely demonic. Or the Dark Fae bilge you guys assumed from the beginning. Their special power is the ability to mimic others.

The second presence registered when I acknowledged there was no way to know what the creature was without closer inspection. The second being was prone on the grass. At first blush, they weren't engaged in a torrid love affair in the middle of an empty park. I was basing that assumption entirely on the malevolence choking me.

Walk away! I tried to turn, but my feet wouldn't obey. There was someone in danger in the park, and I could do something about it. With a curse, I tiptoed into the area. The beast hovering over its victim turned scarlet eyes on me.

My chest started burning as adrenaline dumped into my bloodstream. Specifically the bird on my chest. It was on fire and taking my breath away. Before I passed out, energy sizzled to the surface of the blood racing through my veins. It supercharged me, making me feel powerful.

"Took you long enough," the creature announced in a voice that sounded like metal grinding against stone.

I cast a quick glance around, searching for another enemy. Nothing moved, but I didn't dare take my eyes off the demonic being much longer. "What do you mean?" His statement made the hairs on the back of my neck stand on end. His comment insinuated he was waiting for me, which seemed ridiculous.

"You smell sweet. Far tastier than this pathetic excuse." He kicked the being with a foot as he stood up to his full height of over six feet tall. He had dark hair, caramel skin and was dressed all in black. His clothing looked more like liquid silk. It moved over his body and made me think of a snake.

My stomach turned as he licked his lips. It wasn't a sensuous gesture. Instead, it shouted hunger and the desire to devour every ounce of my being. "I've been looking for you ever since your presence popped up three days ago." He tilted his head. "Something is missing. You're not all there." He sniffed the air.

I swallowed bile and tried to shut down my gag reflex. Once the watery mouth started, I was a goner. I'd vomit, and I couldn't afford to leave myself exposed like that. Analyzing his statement helped.

We had returned from Eidothea three days ago. I was certain he was the one killing in our town for months now. Why was it a few days ago I had sparked his interest? My hand crept up to the burning bird then fell away. I had no idea what was wrong with me or if that is what caught his attention, and I didn't care.

"If you're hunting me, you're doing a piss poor job of it. I had no idea you were even here." Taunting the demon doesn't seem like the best idea, Vi. "Leave me alone." I tried to infuse my voice with the siren traits of my ancestors. I didn't have that much siren in me and had never wished for more until that moment.

"My messages were pretty clear. Perhaps, you're slow. Or, you just don't know how to interpret dreams." My heart stopped when he said that.

I had been plagued with nightmares of my friends being torn apart by a hungry monster with red eyes. He looked nothing like the guy before me. I wondered if he wore human skin to hide his horns and grey skin. Had he sent me the dreams?

A part of me was drawn to him, and my feet were moving before I knew it was happening. I stopped myself a few feet away and got a better look at the person on the ground. It was Faye. One of the witch elders.

Bile filled the back of my throat. Her stomach was cut open, and I could see the ripples of her intestines. They glistened in the moonlight, and her chest didn't rise and fall that I could see. Oh, Goddess. She couldn't be dead.

"Your messages are pathetically cliched. Death is expected from demons and not attractive in the least."

His smile was revolting and almost made me lose control over my stomach. "Good thing all I want is your power." I wondered if it was really Fiona that he was hunting. He might have zeroed in on me because I was connected to her.

I needed to ask Aislinn if she was experiencing anything out of the ordinary. Perhaps that was why she'd been sick lately.

I called up my power. It surged when I called. The winds whipped around me, sending the demon's dark hair flying around his handsome face. I wanted to cry when a blast at him and catch him off-guard.

The rain started next, and the ground rolled beneath our feet. I had to brace myself, so I didn't fall over. The elements raged harder as my heart rate increased. The two seemed connected. That frightened me more than the demon. The elements shouldn't respond to me like that. Witches used the elements, and we drew upon their power. But we weren't able to control them. And we certainly didn't influence them.

The demon glanced around as he tried to shield his face from the rain and wind. I took deep breaths and tried to calm my fear and rage. The more I felt, the more the elements raged. I had to get control of this and fast.

Power filled my chest, making it feel close to bursting. I shook my hands and imagined flinging the terror away from me. Energy flowed from the ends of my hands like sparks from a firework.

They landed on the ground and started fires. The winds continued, but the rain stopped. The tiny lightning bolts continued to fly from my fingertips. I wasn't able to control the power from leaking from me like I was a sieve.

One bolt hit the demon in the chest, leaving a gaping hole in its wake. Black blood dribbled down his chest as he screamed. He batted at his injury and backed away from me. His red eyes wide, and his face pinched from pain. He gave me one last look and took off.

I didn't have time to consider the energy still pouring from me. I landed on my knees next to Faye and groped for a pulse. There was nothing for several seconds. I cried out when a pulse beat beneath my probing fingers. It was barely there.

I looked around for my phone and saw it next to my purse. "I'm getting you help, Faye. Hang on."

I crawled toward my phone as fast as possible. There was no telling if the demon was coming back, but I didn't want to take any chances. I needed to get in touch with Gardoss and call Zreegy to help Faye.

The cold glass in my hand was a lifeline. I flipped it open and hit Zreegy's contact info.

Her smiling face appeared on the screen. "Hey, Violet. Did Fiona burn herself again?"

"No," I burst out. "I'm at the park, and I stumbled across a demon attacking Faye. Her stomach was sliced open. I can see her guts, and her heart is barely beating, and I'm not sure she's breathing. She needs help!"

Zreegy's eyes flared, and she was in motion. "I'll be right there. Put pressure on the wound to stop the bleeding." The screen went black, then reverted back to my contacts as she hung up.

My thumb hovered over Gardoss's number but never made contact. Something hard struck the back of my head, and I lost my grip on the device before face-planting in the grass. Pain exploded in my skull. Blood dripped down my forehead and into my eyes.

I blinked and saw the demon approach Faye again. Black dots danced across my vision, threatening to take over. It took every ounce of energy I had to try and keep my lids open. The demon's head lifted when I could fight the pull no longer, and I slipped into the darkness.

MIDLIFE WITCHERY
MAGICAL
TWIST
BRENDA TRIM

# AUTHORS' NOTE

Review are like hugs. Sometimes awkward. Always welcome! It would mean the world to me if you can take five minutes and let others know how much you enjoyed my work.

Don't forget to visit my website: www.brendatrim.com and sign up for my newsletter, which is jam-packed with exciting news and monthly giveaways. Also, be sure to visit and like my Facebook page https://www.facebook.com/AuthorBrendaTrim to see my daily posts.

Never allow waiting to become a habit. Live your dreams and take risks. Life is happening now.

DREAM BIG!

XOXO,

Brenda

## OTHER WORKS BY BRENDA TRIM

**The Dark Warrior Alliance**

Dream Warrior (Dark Warrior Alliance, Book 1)
Mystik Warrior (Dark Warrior Alliance, Book 2)
Pema's Storm (Dark Warrior Alliance, Book 3)
Isis' Betrayal (Dark Warrior Alliance, Book 4)
Deviant Warrior (Dark Warrior Alliance, Book 5)
Suvi's Revenge (Dark Warrior Alliance, Book 6)
Mistletoe & Mayhem (Dark Warrior Alliance, Novella)
Scarred Warrior (Dark Warrior Alliance, Book 7)
Heat in the Bayou (Dark Warrior Alliance, Novella, Book 7.5)
Hellbound Warrior (Dark Warrior Alliance, Book 8)
Isobel (Dark Warrior Alliance, Book 9)
Rogue Warrior (Dark Warrior Alliance, Book 10)
Shattered Warrior (Dark Warrior Alliance, Book 11)
King of Khoth (Dark Warrior Alliance, Book 12)
Ice Warrior (Dark Warrior Alliance, Book 13)
Fire Warrior (Dark Warrior Alliance, Book 14)
Ramiel (Dark Warrior Alliance, Book 15)

Rivaled Warrior (Dark Warrior Alliance, Book 16)

Dragon Knight of Khoth (Dark Warrior Alliance, Book 17)

Ayil (Dark Warrior Alliance, Book 18)

Guild Master (Dark Alliance Book 19)

Maven Warrior (Dark Alliance Book 20)

Sentinel of Khoth (Dark Alliance Book 21)

Araton (Dark Warrior Alliance Book 22)

Cambion Lord Araton (Dark Warrior Alliance Book 23)

Omega (Dark Warrior Alliance Book 24)

**Dark Warrior Alliance Boxsets:**

Dark Warrior Alliance Boxset Books 1-4

Dark Warrior Alliance Boxset Books 5-8

Dark Warrior Alliance Boxset Books 9-12

Dark Warrior Alliance Boxset Books 13-16

Dark Warrior Alliance Boxset Books 17-20

**Hollow Rock Shifters:**

Captivity, Hollow Rock Shifters Book 1

Safe Haven, Hollow Rock Shifters Book 2

Alpha, Hollow Rock Shifters Book 3

Ravin, Hollow Rock Shifters Book 4

Impeached, Hollow Rock Shifters Book 5

Anarchy, Hollow Rock Shifters Book 6

**Midlife Witchery:**

Magical New Beginnings Book 1

Mind Over Magical Matters Book 2

Magical Twist Book 3

**Bramble's Edge Academy:**

Unearthing the Fae King

Masking the Fae King
Revealing the Fae King

**Midnight Doms:**

Her Vampire Bad Boy
Her Vampire Suspect

Printed in Great Britain
by Amazon

59439822R00139